D1246278

PENANCE FOR THE DEAD

A BOW STREET DUCHESS MYSTERY

BOOK FOUR

CARA DEVLIN

First Cup Press

Copyright © 2023 by Cara Devlin

All rights reserved.

No part of this book may be reproduced in any form or by any electronic or
mechanical means, including information storage and retrieval systems,
without written permission from the author, except for the use of brief
quotations in a book review.

Any references to historical events, real people, or real places are used
fictitiously. Names and characters are products of the author's imagination.

Paperback ISBN: 979-8987612569

CHAPTER ONE

March 1820

SATURDAY NIGHT

T he stale, stuffy air inside Lady Reed's ballroom reeked of floral perfume, cologne, and dank under notes of sweat. Audrey fluttered her silk fan in rapid beats in front of her face, attempting to disburse the overpowering scents. Outside, winter clung on with freezing temperatures and icy gales, and while she didn't particularly care for the blustery cold, shed would have happily leaped into a snow drift right then if it meant escaping the ballroom—and the presence of Lady Minerva Dutton.

The dowager countess had been valiantly attempting to corner Audrey and Philip, the Duke and Duchess of Fournier, and Philip's younger sister, Lady Cassandra, ever since the three of them arrived at the soiree. Knowing the older woman's penchant for gossip and for making thinly veiled cuts, Audrey had tucked Cassie close to her side and weaved between guests to evade her. Cassie had only returned to London a few weeks ago. She'd spent the last several months in Sweden with some of Philip's trusted friends—Mr. and Mrs. Olsson, one of Philip's former Cambridge professors and his wife, who had moved back to Stockholm. They had graciously taken in Cassie when she'd found herself in a dire situation last summer. Unwed and with child, she had needed a place to have her baby, far away from the eyes and ears of polite society. Should anyone learn of her predicament, she would have been thoroughly ruined.

Unfortunately, Lady Dutton was as keen as a hawk when it came to spotting scandals, and Cassie's absence had sparked the countess's interest. Though the soiree was something of a crush, and she'd successfully eluded Lady Dutton for the past half hour, Audrey's luck ran out at the punch table. For the last several minutes, the countess had not relinquished her hold.

"But enough about this party's ill-advised décor," she trilled after commenting at length on Lady Reed's decision to outfit the four corners of the ballroom to reflect the four seasons. "My dear Lady Cassandra, I am still waiting to hear how your aunt is faring."

Cassie, who slipped a little closer to her elder brother, gave no reply. She seemed to freeze under the woman's scrutiny. Philip had sipped his punch slowly during the woman's tiresome monologue on proper ballroom décor, his expression impassive. Now, he cleared his throat.

"Our aunt has made a full recovery, thank you for inquiring," he said.

Cassie had, allegedly, forgone the Little Season last fall to remain in Scotland with her ailing great aunt.

Lady Dutton flashed a grin. "I'm so relieved to hear as much, Your Grace. Tell me, Lady Cassandra, did you have any opportunity to socialize while you were there? I recall Lord

Hartford saying he and his family were in Edinburgh for Michaelmas. Did you not see them?"

Audrey took a sip of her punch and met Philip's glance. By appearances alone, Cassie did not look any different than she had in the summer. However, there was a seriousness to her now that had not been present before. The old Cassie would have waved a hand through the air and spun some excuse with a light laugh and clever remark. This new Cassie looked as dismissive and sour as Philip.

"No," she answered sharply.

Lady Dutton's forehead wrinkled above arching brows.

Audrey smiled, though the expression was wooden. "The duke's aunt resides outside Glasgow. It's rather rustic and out of the way."

"I see," Lady Dutton said. Audrey only hoped the woman did *not* see.

Only family knew the truth; it had been impossible to keep it from Philip's brother Michael, Lord Herrick, and his wife, Genie. Genie would undoubtedly write letters to Cassie in Scotland, to which Aunt Hestia would reply with the truth—that she was not there. And if any of Cassie's friends wrote to her, Aunt Hestia needed to know to redirect the letters to Sweden.

Their dour great aunt had been scandalized, but she'd agreed to protect the family name. Michael had blustered and threatened to kill Lord Renfry, the blackguard who'd seduced and abandoned his sister, but then, like Philip had, he'd grudgingly agreed that keeping the truth from Renfry would benefit them all. The man had stooped to seducing his own stepmothers, the Earl of Bainbury's second and third wives, and neither Philip nor Michael wished for their beloved sister to be married to such an ingrate. Tobias, their youngest sibling still at Cambridge, was the only one who did not know the truth.

Audrey snapped her fan shut. "It is quite a change of pace

3

being back in town after so long in the country," she said, attempting to formulate a reason for her sister-in-law's sullen attitude. "Cassie does so enjoy the fresh air."

Cassie forced an anemic response. "Yes, it is quite overwhelming here."

Audrey's chest tightened with sympathy. Cassie had not said much about the birth of her daughter, or of handing her newborn over to Mrs. Olsson, who'd found a loving home for the child, but she was clearly heartbroken. And seeing Genie and Michael's new baby, George, had likely been salt in a wound. Little George, now nearly five months old, was a round-cheeked, black-haired angel, and even Audrey was not immune to pangs of maternal longing when she held him.

Lady Dutton simpered. "I never marked you as a country girl, Lady Cassandra. Perhaps your newfound love of the countryside is the reason your correspondence while away was so...irregular?"

The letters would have traveled from London, to Scotland, to Sweden and back again, causing quite a delay. It had not gone unnoticed, it seemed.

"Either that or my sister grew weary of dull conversation. A sentiment I share, completely," Philip said, more agitated now.

Lady Dutton's eyes narrowed at his implied barb.

"If you'll excuse us, my lady," he said, and then took Cassie by the arm and stepped away. Audrey quickly followed.

"She won't have anything kind to say about you now," she whispered to Philip once she was by his side again.

"Has she ever?"

"The woman is a wretch," Cassie added, and Audrey could not disagree.

"Perhaps we should take our leave soon," she suggested.

None of them had wanted to attend Lady Reed's soiree to begin with but snubbing one of the most important events of the Season had not been an option. The Duke and Duchess of Fournier hadn't received many invitations during the Little Season, as they'd still been entrenched in scandal. First, Philip had been accused of a gruesome murder, one from which he'd been exonerated, but it had still damaged his reputation. And then, two murders on the grounds of their country home, Fournier Downs, had threatened to drag them back into disgrace. Getting back into society and introducing Cassie properly was expected. With any luck, it would also begin to repair the Fournier name.

But not if Philip continued to be such a bad-tempered bear.

Cassie stopped to say hello to a few ladies she was acquainted with, and Audrey and Philip fell back, near one of the many tall windows lining the walls of the vast room. The glass radiated cold, and Audrey longed to press her cheek against it.

"Are you feeling unwell?" Audrey asked him after a moment.

He had undergone a second mercury salivation treatment the previous week, and it had left him bedridden for three days. His first round of treatment had taken place in November, and though the physician had told him it would completely cure his syphilis, Philip had become unwell in January with what he called a "flare", though he refused to elaborate on the symptoms to Audrey, who needled him out of pure concern. Once he was feeling well again, Dr. Bagley from Lock Hospital had met him for another treatment. He still appeared pale, his cheekbones more prominent than usual.

"I am fine," he replied, then with a sigh, added, "Just a little tired."

Audrey took his arm. To the rest of the *ton* currently in the ballroom, the action would look like a wife taking her husband's arm in loving affection. And while Audrey did love Philip, and he loved her, it was not in the traditional sense. They were the best of friends now that they'd been wed three years. Audrey often wondered if she and Philip might even be closer than many of the married couples surrounding them. So often, people married for alliance, for money, for titles and position. She and Philip had married for convenience, too, but with the mutual understanding that theirs would be a marriage based on friendship. That didn't mean they did not have their hiccups. The one that immediately, and often, came to her mind had a name: Principal Bow Street Officer Hugh Marsden.

It had been several months since she'd seen him, and since they'd been in lockstep while uncovering a deadly blackmailing scheme that involved Audrey and a few of her former acquaintances at Shadewell Sanatorium. When they'd pinned down the culprit and arrested the deranged woman, Hugh had made sure Audrey would not be connected to the asylum in any way. He'd been true to his word. The last five months had been normal to the point of tedium. Considering that his status as a Bow Street officer was leagues below her own rank as duchess, there was no acceptable reason for them to see, or so much as bump into, each other.

She missed him. The yawning ache in her chest whenever she thought of him was proof. Perhaps, if another few months passed, and then a few more, that ache would begin to lessen. Audrey wasn't certain if she looked forward to that, or if she dreaded it.

Her only link to Hugh was through Lord Thornton. She would not have even that had she not grown so weary of daily monotony that she'd decided to attend a scientific lecture at the Lyceum. It wasn't entirely unheard of for ladies to sit in on such lectures, and when she saw an advertisement in the paper for an exhibition and address on fossils of prehistoric sea creatures, she'd been unable to stay away. She'd taken her maid Greer as a formality and had chosen two seats in the back of the hall. The male attendees had all noticed them, of course, and had whispered amongst themselves. When one of them stood and came greet her, Audrey's heart had started racing. Lord Thornton was Hugh's closest friend, and as fourth son of a marquess, had decided to make his way in the world as a physician. He'd welcomed Audrey to the Lyceum and offered to sit with her and Greer, then afterward, introduce her to a few of the more "accepting" men of his acquaintance there.

Audrey had since attended several lectures, and Lord Thornton had been at most of them. He'd discreetly let her know that Hugh's arm, which had been seriously injured in November when they had captured the murderous Miss Delia Montgomery, was recovering nicely. That he was busy as ever at Bow Street, and that Sir, the young street urchin-turned-errand boy who was devoted to Hugh, was also doing well after his own stabbing, also at Delia's hand.

"Come," Philip said now, interrupting her thoughts. "Let us say our goodbyes to Lady Reed."

He and Audrey rejoined with Cassie and then found their hostess near the springtime corner of the ballroom. Garlands of faux green leaves cut from crepe wove through a trellis studded with bright yellow and red silk daffodils. A mass of cottony clouds hung suspended from the ceiling. It was truly garish.

Lady Reed sipped a glass of punch, ignoring the chattering women on either side of her. She stared into the crowd, her brow pinched. In fact, it took the clearing of one of her companion's throats before she noticed the duke and duchess had joined them. With a start, Lady Reed turned to them, blinking.

"Oh, Your Graces, forgive my distraction." She quickly set the punch glass on the tray of a nearby footman. Audrey noticed the slight tremor of her hand, causing the punch to nearly splash over the lip of the glass.

"Is all well, Lady Reed?" Audrey asked. The older

7

marchioness, her steel gray hair stylishly upswept with framing curls, again seemed to startle.

"Yes, quite," she answered shortly before falling awkwardly quiet.

"We wanted to thank you for your hospitality before we take our leave," Audrey said after a moment.

"My wife feels a head ache coming on," Philip said before the marchioness could ask why. Audrey, still holding Philip's arm, covertly pinched him through his evening jacket. She wasn't prone to head aches in the least; however, it was a reasonable excuse.

"Oh, how disappointing," the lady said. If her attention had not roamed toward the crowd again, Audrey might have believed her. But she was clearly distracted. Concerned, even.

"Thank you for attending, Your Graces," she said, her eyes flicking back to the duke, then toward Audrey. "Your Grace, I do hope you are feeling better—"

Lady Reed broke off just as a strange, foul smell wafted under Audrey's nose. Behind them, voices raised with alarm. Audrey turned to find a grayish haze quickly filling the room. Men and women nearby covered their mouths and noses with their gloved hands, coughing.

"What in the world...?" Philip was cut off as he began to hack on a cough too. Audrey covered her own mouth and nose, but the sharp, sulfuric odor of the smoke slipped between her fingers and stung her nostrils.

"Cassie!" Audrey cried as her sister-in-law began to cough wildly. Philip gave his sister his handkerchief and wrapped his arm around her. The crush of guests, panicking now, began to surge toward the ballroom doors. With watering eyes, Audrey pulled on Philip's sleeve to stop him from joining the masses. They would only get bottlenecked at the doors.

"This way!" she shouted above the sudden clamor. Philip

redirected Cassie as he followed Audrey toward the back of the room. A pair of glass doors had been shut against the cold air, though during a stuffy spring soiree, they would have been thrown open to an airy veranda.

Audrey navigated through the thick smoke, her throat beginning to burn, her eyes streaming with tears. She felt a waft of cold air before reaching the veranda doors; they were already open. It seemed she wasn't the only one who'd judged this as a better escape.

However, when she, Philip, and Cassie spilled out onto the veranda, their feet swallowed by an inch of slushy snow, they were entirely alone. Audrey gasped for air, relieved to be free from the smoke, though her throat and eyes still stung. For several moments, they stood by themselves, confused and overwhelmed and shivering. But then, a handful of others found the open veranda doors and joined them. By the looks of their red, teary eyes, everyone else was just as afflicted by the smoke.

"Philip," Audrey gasped, when he doubled over, still coughing. Cassie had quickly recovered and now gripped her brother's arm, rubbing his back as the convulsion passed.

The dozen or so others now shivered in distress, all of them speaking at once.

"Is the ballroom on fire?"

"What was that foul smoke?"

"I think my throat is bleeding!"

The smoke had certainly seared Audrey's throat too, but she didn't taste blood, thankfully. Inside, the smoke was so thick, it indeed looked like something had caught ablaze, but there were no flames, and the smell was not the familiar one of burning wood. It was chemical.

"What a predicament! Now we must walk through the snow, to get to the front of the house," a woman bemoaned.

"I will go around," Philip rasped. "Cassie, Audrey, stay here while I fetch Carrigan. We will carry the two of you—"

"Don't be absurd, it is only snow. We do not need carrying," Cassie said, and Audrey was happy to hear a bit of her high spirit again.

A short, grating scream from inside the ballroom split the air. Everyone on the veranda went quiet. It hadn't been a scream of panic, but of pain and surprise.

No one moved. Audrey, however, could not remain where she stood. Someone had been hurt. Instinct drove her forward. She tore Philip's handkerchief from Cassie's fingers and, covering her nose and mouth, plunged back into the smoke.

"Audrey!" both Philip and Cassie shouted after her. She didn't stop. The smoke engulfed her, but if she squinted, she could peer through it a bit better. It still burned her eyes, but as she hurried deeper into the ballroom, the brume lessened.

A sharp prick of pain in the center of her foot startled her to a stop. She gasped and immediately lifted her foot to see what she had trod upon. Attached to the sole of her slipper was a small metal object. She plucked it out and saw it was a sort of charm—three golden leaves spread out like a fan—and that the sharp post backing it had pierced her foot.

Audrey tossed the offending thing aside and returned to searching the room for the person who had screamed. "Hello? Is someone injured?" she called.

She stopped abruptly again when a figure on the parquet flooring became visible through the smoke. It was a woman. She lay prone on the floor, face down, arms thrown out beside her. She wasn't moving.

"Audrey!" Philip barked, and a moment later, he grabbed her arm. "What the devil are you doing?"

He then saw the woman and swore under his breath. She and Philip approached, but instantly, Audrey knew it was too late. A dark pool of blood had started to creep out from around her torso.

"Help!" Philip called between gasping coughs as Audrey stared at the dead woman in shocked horror. "Someone, quick! A woman is hurt, help!"

Audrey snapped out of her shock and quickly kneeled beside the woman. Her face was turned, her cheek to the floor. Her eyes were half open, but flat. She was certainly dead. *Killed.*

Within seconds of Philip's shout, men came forward through the dispersing haze. Before the oncoming men could see her, Audrey reached for the woman's hand. With her gloved hand, she slipped off the simple ring the woman wore on her right center finger.

"*Audrey*," Philip warned under his breath, knowing exactly what she was doing.

With the ring, Audrey could apply her most unusual ability to read the memories of objects, to see into their recent past. Perhaps she could find out who had hurt this poor woman. It had to have been someone at the soiree. The smoke...had it been a trick to clear out the room and set upon her, unseen?

She closed her fingers around the ring and stood as several men, including Lord Reed, joined them. Philip pulled her close to his side.

"We heard a scream from the veranda," he explained. "Her Grace and I found her like this."

Lord Reed bent to peer at the dead woman. "Beckett," he called sharply to another man with him. "Send for a constable at Bow Street."

Audrey's heart slowed, then streamed out a few extra beats. But then Philip spoke, stilling her pulse.

"It would be best if the officer you fetched was someone other than Officer Marsden," he said to Lord Reed.

Audrey turned to gape at him. "Why would you say that?"

He couldn't possibly want to restrict Hugh from this crime just to keep him from her presence.

"Quite right," Lord Reed said gravely. "If I'm not mistaken, this is Lady Eloisa Neatham."

Gooseflesh rode up Audrey's arms and down her spine. She stared at the dead woman with new shock. Eloisa Neatham left London years ago after a salacious scandal, in which her half-brother was accused of ruining her.

And her half-brother was none other than Officer Hugh Marsden.

CHAPTER
TWO

Hugh thought he would never see her again.

Outside, the dense gray clouds broke apart and bright afternoon sunlight streamed through the windows of his study. The rays touched her shoulders and hair, the backlit glow almost making her appear as a heavenly apparition.

But, no, she was real. Basil had just announced her, and in she had walked...looking nearly the same as she had six years ago, when Hugh had last seen her.

"Eloisa." Her name came out little more than a whisper.

Hugh's half-sister, who was four years his junior, wore a simple maroon cloak, gloves, and a matching velvet bonnet. Her lips started to form a smile, but then it wobbled and fell flat.

"Hugh. It is good to see you again." Her voice was strained, revealing her nervousness. She clasped her gloved hands in front of her, a reticule hanging from her wrist by silk strings.

He stood motionless in front of his desk, his whole body having gone numb when she appeared. Now, his blood started to pump again, giving him back his wits.

"What are you doing here?" he asked. Then, "Where have you been?"

Rumors had circulated, saying she'd gone to America, but considering his lack of contact with his two half-brothers, Bartholomew and Thomas, he'd never been sure. All he knew for certain was that nearly six years ago, Eloisa had left London after a horrendous scandal erupted within the Neatham household. Bartholomew, Hugh's elder half-brother, had accused Hugh of ruining her. It was utterly false, and Barty knew it. But the young viscount, newly titled as Lord Neatham after the death of their father, had not cared. The accusation was made, publicly, followed by a challenge to a duel. Eloisa's honor would be upheld. And Barty would get what he'd always wanted: Hugh gone, one way or another.

Even though he'd been the late viscount's by-blow, Hugh had been raised within the Neatham household, given the same education, the same care as the viscount's legitimate children. Some might say Hugh had been given more care than the others. He himself had often felt smug with the thought. His father had loved him; he had also cared enough for Hugh's mother to instate her as the children's nanny. When Thomas, the youngest and only one year apart from Eloisa, no longer needed a nanny, Hugh's mother had been given a living and comfortable rooms right in town. The viscount hadn't shunted her off into the country to be forgotten. The care he'd shown had inspired an undercurrent of envy and malcontent from Barty, the heir, but Hugh hadn't seen the catastrophic accusation coming.

It had made shooting his half-brother in the arm during the duel, rendering it permanently useless, almost gratifying. Barty, of course, would have sent his bullet straight into Hugh's heart, had he been a better shot.

Eloisa stepped forward and drew a visibly bracing breath. "I have come on an urgent matter. I hope this is not an inconvenient time?"

Hugh clenched his molars. What had been at first shock was now turning to low, simmering anger. "Inconvenient? How kind of you to inquire."

She pursed her lips, as if accepting the barb. Expecting it, even. She had not aged by much; her hair was still a glossy auburn, much like her mother's, the late Lady Neatham, though it was styled less fashionably than Eloisa ever would have worn it before. In fact, she appeared rather plain, like a member of the gentry or working class.

"Does Bartholomew know you are in town?" he asked, guessing that her intention with such simple clothing was to go unnoticed.

She quickly shook her head. "No. No, I haven't spoken to him in years. Thomas, either."

Hugh frowned, wondering if he should believe her. "How many years would that be?"

"Several." Eloisa took a furtive look over her shoulder, toward the windows overlooking Bedford Street. The drapes were open, but it was unlikely anyone was standing outside, gawping through the glass. "Not since I returned from France, five years ago."

"I thought you were in America," Hugh said.

Her reputation had been destroyed, alongside Hugh's. He'd often wondered why Barty had not considered that before calling Hugh out in front of a crowd of men at the boxing club they'd both belonged to at the time. There had been other avenues Barty could have taken, and yet he'd selected a glaringly public one.

By then, Hugh had already been gone from Neatham House for a year or so. His father had left him a generous living, allowing him a gentleman's lifestyle, even if he wasn't titled. Barty had wanted to destroy Hugh, certainly, but his own sister too? It had never made much sense.

Eloisa shook her head. "No. Barty chose France. He knew of a place where I could..." She seemed to wilt. "There was to be a baby."

Hugh cringed. Thought he might be ill. A baby. *Christ.* He turned from her and snatched the whisky decanter from his desk.

"And Barty wanted you out of sight," he murmured as he poured himself a larger than usual amount.

Lady Cassandra, the Duke of Fournier's sister, had been in the same sticky situation last summer and fall. She'd gone to live with the duke's friends. Hugh doubted his half-brother had been as kind to Eloisa.

"What sort of place was it?" he asked, thinking of Shadewell, an institution in Northumberland where those of "quality" could send their dirty little secrets.

"Does it matter?" Eloisa asked.

"No, I suppose not."

He'd visited Shadewell in the fall with Audrey Sinclair, the Duchess of Fournier, while investigating a blackmailing and murder case. The asylum was where she had been sent for two years by her mother and uncle for possessing the incredible, if intolerable, ability to read the memories of individual objects.

Over the winter, Hugh had caught himself countless times looking at something like a paperweight or pocket watch, a necklace or a doorknob, and wondering what they might show

Audrey if she were to hold them in her hand. He thought of her far too often.

Ending his arrangement with Miss Gloria Hanson had been the right thing to do; though she did not love Hugh, she deserved better than simply being a vessel for Hugh to slake his lust while he harbored a growing affection for the duchess. His arrangement with Gloria ended amicably and since then, he'd mostly been alone. Grant Thornton's sister's friend had been a willing distraction a few times, though only after acknowledging and agreeing that it would be nothing more than that. Still, the few encounters had left him unsatisfied.

He was beginning to think any woman who was not Audrey would.

"Where is the child now?" he asked Eloisa.

In a flat tone, she answered, "There is no child. She was stillborn."

His first thought was cruel—that it was probably for the best. Hugh didn't offer condolences. Even though he had always liked Eloisa the most out of his three half-siblings, resentment toward her lingered. She had left him to ruination, turning her back on him and the lies Barty perpetuated. Certainly, she could not have stayed in London with an increasing middle. In truth, Hugh wasn't sure what more she could have possibly done to help him. At the time, it surely had not been her priority.

"Tell me why you are here," Hugh said, his patience and the novelty of seeing her again after so long wearing thin.

"I want to hire you," she answered. "Privately."

He sipped from his glass, peering at her from over the rim. He let a moment pass while he tried to comprehend the statement. "You know I work for Bow Street?"

"Yes."

She'd been in contact with someone here in London, then. A

friend? She'd had many, but after the scandal, they'd have cut her completely. At the time, Barty had not been married, so it wouldn't be his wife, Lila.

"I have a full case load already." He set down his glass and avoided her eyes. "I can refer you to another officer."

"No. That won't work. It needs to be you."

"I can't help you." He'd already tried once. Look where that had got him: painted by all and sundry as a villain of the worst ilk. He'd worked these last six years to build a life where the duel with Barty and the lurid accusations weren't the first things people would think of when they heard his name.

"If you won't help me, then at least help yourself!" Eloisa said, her voice rising but not in strength. There was panic there, desperation. He peered at her, growing curious.

"What do you mean by that?"

Soft lines around her dark brown eyes tensed. She attempted to calm herself. "You aren't the only one who despises Barty. Whatever you may think of me, however you may hate me—"

"I don't hate you."

"I was a coward."

"You were scared." The resentment he'd held onto for so long now flagged. In a rush, he admitted that Eloisa didn't deserve it. She was as much a victim as he was. "Barty is the coward. As is Thomas."

"Don't. Please." She shook her head as if to dislodge the names from her ears. With another furtive look over her shoulders, through the front windows, she came back to her reason for being here. "I want you to find someone."

"I'm not a private inquiry agent."

"You'll want to find her," she insisted, looking and sounding more confident than she'd been since walking through his front door.

Hugh relented, though not without a vexed sigh. "Who?"

"Miss April Barlow."

He had never heard of her before. Hugh crossed his arms and stopped himself from saying no again. For whatever reason, Eloisa was here, after many years, and she looked afraid of being caught by their brother. That alone interested him enough to ask, "And who is this Miss April Barlow?"

She held his eyes and answered, "Your mother."

CHAPTER
THREE

Gnawing stomach cramps plagued Audrey the morning after the murder. Considering Philip and Cassie were in their rooms, each of them suffering from the same symptoms, she deduced the chemical haze released into the ballroom the evening before was the cause. Either that, or the minted mackerel hors d'oeuvres Lady Reed had served had been spoiled. Either way, the ill feeling had capped off a wretched evening.

The hot bath that Greer had drawn for her had eased some of the cramping, and the slippery elm tea their cook, Mrs. Comstock had insisted they all sip had done much to soothe their raw throats. If only there was something that could be done to take away the images Lady Eloisa Neatham's ring had funneled into Audrey's mind.

Late last night, she, Philip, and Cassie had returned to Violet House after spending more than an hour trapped at Lord and

Lady Reed's home, going over the events with Bow Street officials. None of the constables or officers had been Hugh, just as
Philip had advised. Calling him in to investigate his own sister's
death would have been unprofessional, and what with the old
scandal, how could he remain impartial?

Audrey had told herself that she was grateful he didn't
come; if she'd seen him, all the work she had done building up
the walls around herself to keep out thoughts and feelings for
Hugh Marsden would have likely come tumbling down. All he'd
have to do would be to walk through the doors, meet her eyes,
and say hello.

Instead, she'd given her statement to a man named Officer
Tyne. The officer had snapped his eyes to hers in recognition
when Lord Reed had introduced her and Philip. Hugh had told
her back in the autumn that there were some at Bow Street who
called Audrey "his duchess" due to the notorious case in April,
when she'd run her own investigation contrary to Hugh's into
Miss Lovejoy's murder, and again in August, when she'd sent an
official request for him to come to Hertfordshire for another
murder investigation. Last November, they had worked
together again, which had probably not gone unnoticed by his
colleagues.

Officer Tyne had graciously said nothing and sketched
down their account of hearing the scream, running into the
chemical smoke, and finding the body. Of course, she didn't
reveal that she had Eloisa's ring in her ballgown's pocket.
Always having despised the feeling of having a reticule's strings
tied around her wrist, Audrey opted to have pockets sewn into
all her gowns and dresses. It also proved far easier to slip something into the folds of her skirts than into a reticule.

In her own room at Violet House, she'd transferred the ring
to the drawer of her bedside table. After her bath, Greer left her
for the night, and Audrey had gathered her courage before

holding the ring and opening her mind to what it would show her.

Pushing past the most recent images of herself taking the ring, she dove backward; it was almost like stretching out her arms and parting a thick mist. Only, this time, it was the gray haze of the ballroom. Eloisa had been running through it, turning to glance over her shoulder time and again, as if someone was pursuing her. But in the smoke, Audrey saw no one.

Further back, before the smoky haze filled Eloisa's vision, the air was clear and dark, lit only by the flame of a single taper. Lady Reed's tense, lined face had filled her vision. The marchioness looked straight into Eloisa's eyes and shook her head resolutely. "No. I'm sorry, but *no*."

The lady wasn't angry; she appeared nervous.

"You must leave. You cannot be here," she added, the muted, underwater sound of her voice ebbing from the vision.

The strength of the memories weakened, and the vision went dark. Setting the ring upon the bedside table, she made a promise to get the piece back to Eloisa one way or another.

At the soiree, Audrey had noted Lady Reed's distraction. By that point, she had already seen and spoken to Eloisa. Why then, had she insisted to Officer Tyne that she'd had no idea Eloisa was in her home?

Audrey still pondered that thought as morning wore toward afternoon. Her stomachache had not abated, but she decided to go down for a late breakfast.

"Cassie is still quite upset," Philip announced as she entered the breakfast room, favoring her right foot. The sole throbbed a little from where the gold leaf charm had pierced her slipper the previous night. But she would not complain. It was inconsequential compared to the mortal injury Lady Eloisa had suffered.

Philip was already seated at the table, his plate nearly cleared. "I cannot blame her," he added. "It seems every time we turn around, there is a dead body in our path."

Audrey sat down, the footman, Harris, pushing the seat in for her. She smiled a thank you to the servant and spread her napkin onto her lap. "Surely not every time we turn around."

Philip merely speared her with a look that needed no words.

"Very well, I admit it *is* highly unusual. However, what are we to do about it?" Audrey was in earnest with the question. It wasn't as if she elected to find recently murdered people. Although, she couldn't deny the odd longing she'd felt over the last few months to put her mind to work investigating *some* criminal case. She missed the excitement and challenge.

Philip turned toward Harris and told him that would be all for now. The footman gave a short bow and left the breakfast room.

"Cassie has already been through so much this year," Philip said, lowering his voice. The footman would be just outside, awaiting a summons.

Audrey sipped her tea, considering an idea that had come to her when Cassie had shown apathy after arriving home. "Do you think Cassie would like to visit your Aunt Hestia in Scotland —in truth this time? She seems so unhappy. Perhaps she needs a little more time before rejoining society."

Even as she said it, she knew it would be impossible. Cassie had already been away too long. Lady Dutton's prying questions at the soiree had proved as much. To send her away again would only inspire more gossip, more questions. It would only draw more attention to the Fournier name as well—something they had been trying to avoid. In vain, it seemed.

As Philip mentioned these same reasons against a visit to Scotland, Audrey speared a sausage with her fork, then laid the fork down. She wasn't hungry. Her stomach felt like a churning abyss, though not solely because of the smoke from last night. Cassie's predicament concerned her. Would the poor girl ever recover from giving her child up to another couple? Or would thoughts of the infant forever haunt her, lingering in the back of her mind, even when she did find a man to marry and build a family with?

Philip had at first suggested that he and Audrey adopt the child. Audrey could have spent several months away, ostensibly in confinement, before returning with the child, acting as if she had born it herself. But Audrey had refused. She would never feel like the child's mother, not with Cassie always there, knowing the truth and pretending she didn't feel an unbreakable attachment.

Now, however, Cassie would never see her child again, and Audrey felt slightly guilty that she had turned down Philip's proposal.

"Are you listening to me?"

Audrey blinked and looked up from her still full plate. "I'm sorry, did you say something?"

He gave her a flat look. Then, with a shake of his head and a deep breath, he reached for the newssheet, folded on the table next to his cup of tea.

"I said, there is something I need to show you." Philip tapped his fingers on the folded morning edition of the *Times*, but then hesitated.

"What is it?" Audrey eyed the paper under his hand.

Every paper in London would have gone to press with the news of Lady Eloisa Neatham's murder. No doubt, each one would mention the old scandal involving Hugh. Audrey had prepared herself for it, though so far that morning, she had yet to see a newssheet.

"Promise me you will not do anything rash." Philip's dark

green eyes bore into hers, awaiting an answer. He was entirely serious. Dread pooled in her stomach.

"You have me worried, Philip."

"Promise me," he repeated.

Audrey hitched her chin. "I promise to think before I act."

It was the most he was going to get from her. He relented and handed over the newssheet. She smoothed it out and took in the headline. Her body went cold, and her lungs ceased working.

> *Ruined Daughter of Viscount Slain*
> *Accused Bow Street Runner Missing*

She couldn't read the first few inches of the article fast enough. Her eyes scraped over the print, then she forced herself to go back to the start and begin again, this time slower. Her heart knocked against her ribs as she read, her eyes skimming over the expected reminders of Hugh's accused role in Eloisa's ruination, as well as the duel in which Bartholomew, Viscount Neatham, had been shot in the arm. Though dueling was now against the law, it hadn't been six years ago. Duels had been a matter of honor, of revenge and justice. The article certainly made the viscount out to be the wronged party, and Hugh, the villain.

However, her eyes clung to the type that discussed the events of the previous evening:

Bow Street's Principal Officer Hugh Marsden is accused of invading Viscount Neatham's home on Kensington Square just past nine o'clock yesterday evening. Mr. Marsden reportedly attacked the lord in his study, and after a brief struggle with the staff, fled on foot. Less than an hour later, the lord's sister, Lady Eloisa Neatham, absent from London these last several years, was stabbed to death on the ballroom floor of Lord Reed's home. A fireless smoke had prompted guests at the soiree to flee. Lady Eloisa was discovered by the Duke and Duchess of Fournier. The police are searching for Mr. Marsden in connection to both attacks.

Audrey slapped the paper down. "This is preposterous! Why on earth would Hugh attack Lord Neatham in his home? He certainly would not kill his sister! You know him, Philip. He isn't a murderer."

Her husband sat placidly in his chair, his hands folded on the table before him. "I know he is not. But he has gotten himself into a pickle by forcing his way into Neatham's home and attacking him."

"Allegedly," Audrey reminded.

Philip gestured toward the paper. "If you read the whole article, you'll see that the police were summoned to Neatham's home *before* the murder took place at the soiree. They are not making up the attack to further incriminate Mr. Marsden in the murder."

Audrey hadn't read the whole article. She didn't know if she could stomach it. Why would Hugh have gone to his half-brother's home in the first place? He despised Lord Neatham for the accusations he'd made and the challenge to a duel that had forced Hugh to defend himself. He hadn't wanted to kill Bartholomew then. What would drive him to become so unhinged and murderous now?

"He is missing, Audrey," Philip added, gently. "The attack on Neatham and then the murder immediately afterward... It doesn't look good now that he has fled."

Audrey shoved back her chair and stood, the need to move, to do something, burning through her limbs.

"Where are you going?" Philip asked.

"I don't know." Her mind whirled, and her pulse wouldn't steady. Where would Hugh have gone? Why would he have run?

"You promised you would do nothing rash," Philip said, pushing back his chair as well.

"I promised I would think before acting," she replied, "and that is what I am doing."

The news article painted Hugh as a deranged murderer, linking the past scandal to this new one. But those who knew Hugh would know that he wasn't capable of something so heinous. Lord Thornton immediately came to mind. He was Hugh's closest friend, and he possessed a fine home, large enough in which to hide. Surely, Bow Street would have gone there first—his friendship with the physician was well known. But Lord Thornton did not have to allow them inside.

"Let the officials solve this," Philip said firmly. He then lowered his voice again, thoughtful of Harris just outside the breakfast room door. "I know you care for Marsden, but if you defend him publicly, there will be consequences for *all* of us."

She snapped her eyes to his, annoyance zinging through her. Once again, Philip's concern for their standing in society reared its ugly head. The near destruction of his own good name last spring had left him perpetually fretful over how the rest of the ton viewed them. However, if she were being totally honest, it was an evergreen concern of his. Hiding who he was from those who would turn their backs on him had been his primary concern for much longer than a year.

"How I feel about Hugh is irrelevant," she said, though she couldn't look Philip in the eye while saying it. "What matters is that the wrong person is being hunted for Lady Eloisa's murder. This article and others like it are going to work the public up into a froth over Hugh, while the real murderer gets away."

Philip stepped back from his chair and approached her, softening his voice even more. "What did it show you?" he asked. Then, arching a dark blond brow, added, "The ring you took."

27

He'd seen her, of course, and had known what she planned to do with it. However, last night he had not come through the boudoir attaching their two sets of rooms to demand to know the results. He might not have been feeling well enough. Or perhaps he'd wanted to ignore his wife's meddling habits.

"Just smoke," she said, then clamped her mouth shut before she could say more.

Eloisa's strange conversation with Lady Reed proved that Lady Reed had lied to Officer Tyne. Finding out why was Audrey's natural first step in sorting out all this madness. Restlessness stole over her again. Worry for Hugh did as well. If he was found and arrested, he would be as deeply in trouble as Philip had been last April. But Hugh would not have a peerage title as a layer of protection. The thought chilled her heart.

Philip crossed his arms, the corners of his mouth turning down in thought. "What are you going to do?"

The question took her off guard. She peered at him, speechless for a moment. Her mind scrambled for at least a half-truth.

"I'm going to speak to Lady Reed," she said. "I can return the ring. Perhaps I can say I found it on the floor and meant to give it to her the night before but became distracted by all the commotion."

The marchioness would undoubtedly be plagued with callers today; Audrey's arrival would not be noted as anything out of the ordinary.

Philip must have agreed. Instead of arguing and telling her to stay at Violet House or anywhere else not associated with the murder, he took out his fob watch to peer at the time. "Very well. I suppose that won't be seen as too out of the ordinary. I must go. There is a session at the House I am required to sit for."

He put away his watch and arched a brow at her. "I will do everything in my power to help Marsden, should he need it. I promise you that."

She believed him, but she also knew that Philip's power would only stretch so far.

He bid her a good morning and left the breakfast room with a purposeful stride. Audrey nibbled her bottom lip with a twinge of guilt. She hadn't been entirely truthful with him. Lady Reed's home was her destination, and she would indeed return the ring. However, she was not planning to leave the marchioness's presence until she'd confessed to seeing Eloisa last night and explaining why she'd lied about it.

If Hugh couldn't investigate this murder himself, Audrey would do it for him. And she would not stop until she proved him innocent.

CHAPTER
FOUR

Friday Morning

The morning after Eloisa's unexpected visit to number 19 Bedford Street, Hugh rose before dawn. With a few pounding knocks upon Basil's door, he roused his perpetually dour valet from sleep with an order to hire a chaise and have it ready as soon as possible.

"It is four o'clock in the morning," Basil replied, still attempting to insert his arm into the sleeve of his dressing grown. "What could be so bloody important?"

"I have a clock of my own, Basil, I know the time." He was used to his valet's cheek, which would have certainly gotten him sacked had he been employed in any other household. "I need to be on the road to Surrey by the time the sun rises."

Basil mumbled some inaudible complaint and closed the door.

Hugh descended into the kitchen where the fire in the grate had long since gone out overnight. Mrs. Peets would arrive just

30

past five to begin breakfast and prepare a dinner that Basil could easily heat in the stove that evening. Employing a live-in cook wasn't necessary for a bachelor, and neither was having a live-in maid. Greta came three days a week to tidy. Basil contained himself to the wash, which was a point of pride for him.

Far more useful was the scrappy and smelly Sir. The boy had proved himself to be incredibly valuable, and not just for running messages and carrying out simple tasks. Sir had an eye for detail and a hawk-like instinct, and he always knew when he could be of use. After he'd nearly been killed last autumn, stabbed and left for dead while out on a task, Hugh worried Sir's mother would no longer allow him to come around. Instead, the opposite happened: Mrs. Givens had come to Hugh and asked if Sir—or rather, Davy—could spend more time on Bedford Street, assisting him. The work was good for him, she said, and it kept him out of the house. It wasn't always safe there, she added, hesitantly. "You saw the bruises," she'd whispered. Hugh had. The boy's body had been riddled with old and new marks, compliments of Sir's drunken brute of a father. There wasn't much Hugh could do to curb the man's temper; he held no authority when it came to another man's wife and children. However, he could offer Sir a refuge, and so that's what he did.

He brought his fist down upon the door to a small room off the kitchen. It was little more than a broom closet, but even getting Sir to accept that had been a trial. When Hugh had told Sir that he was ordering him to either move into Bedford Street or find other employment, the lad had reacted just as Hugh had anticipated: he'd hollered and griped and threatened to find another Bow Street officer to assist before storming off. The next day, he'd shown up at the kitchen door with a single sack in his hand and a scowl on his lips.

"I ain't sharing no room with Baz."

"Basil would rather lick clean his tin of boot black before sharing a room with you," Hugh replied, suppressing a grin of victory.

"I come and go as I please," Sir had said next.

"Do I look like your nanny?" Hugh had shot back. Then held up his pointer finger. "You don't touch my liquor. Not one drop, do you hear me?"

He didn't for a moment think that Sir would touch the liquor in the house, but he couldn't appear to be too accommodating.

"The stuff tastes like shite anyhow," Sir scoffed, sauntering into the kitchen, and immediately throwing open the door to the broom closet. It was mostly empty, excepting a few spider webs. "I'll take this spot."

Hugh told him to drag down the bed from the guest room upstairs and to stay out of the pudding Mrs. Peets had made for that night's dinner. He'd left Sir to his own devices, suspecting the boy had been thinking about claiming that broom closet as a room for some time.

Now, the door swung open on its creaky hinges and Sir, fully dressed, stood at attention. "What's the disaster, Mister Hugh?"

He peered at Sir. "How long have you been awake?"

"Since you was bellowing at Baz upstairs to hire a chaise."

He hadn't realized the floors were so thin. "We're going to Chatham Park in Surrey. Have something to eat, and we'll be on our way."

Hugh turned to leave to make sure Basil had not gone back to sleep.

"This have to do with the lady who showed up yesterday?" Sir asked.

His soles dragged to a stop on the kitchen's stone floor. "Yes," he answered tersely. "Be ready."

Sir wouldn't press for more, and Hugh was grateful for it.

Within the hour, the chaise was delivered, and Basil had kitted Hugh out in something not only appropriate for a meeting with a knight, but also warm enough to withstand the cold while traveling. The chaise had three sides and a roof to block some of the weather, but he and Sir would still need to be bundled. Lord Barrow lived about two hours west of London on an estate known as Chatham Park. It was a relatively small piece of land, though Eloisa had said the knight took great pride in it and lived there year-round, hardly coming up to London at all.

As Hugh and Sir made their way into the sprawling countryside, the four wheels of the chaise slowed by the crunchy ice and mud on the road, Hugh fought the agitated itch that had plagued him all night, ever since Eloisa's departure. *April Barlow*. The name darted around his mind, clashing with another name: Catherine Marsden. His mother.

Catherine was a woman he could put a face to. Memories as well, nearly twenty years of them. At the age of two and thirty, she had been a spinster when she and Viscount Neatham had an affair. Hugh had been the result of their dalliance, but the viscount had not treated Hugh or Catherine with any sort of disdain. Much to the viscountess's displeasure, certainly. No doubt she'd been humiliated by the situation. It wasn't as though he were the only man in the ton to have illegitimate offspring and to take responsibility financially for the mother and child; but he had been more assertive about the care he showed Hugh and Catherine. Some would say too public and bold. Shameless.

Yesterday, Eloisa had confirmed what Hugh already knew: that the late viscountess had been bitterly against Hugh's presence in the household. She'd hated him and Catherine, but more so, she'd hated that her husband had not thrown them both out. It had crippled their marriage, and when the viscountess had died at the relatively young age of six and thirty after a long illness, Barty had placed the blame on Hugh and his mother.

These things all made sense to Hugh. Having grown up within the Neatham household, moving between their homes in London and Surrey, he'd felt the brunt of the viscountess's displeasure and Barty's envy. Thomas and Eloisa, being a few years younger than he and Barty, had simply fallen in line with their elder brother's edicts.

What didn't make an ounce of sense were the things Eloisa told him regarding April Barlow.

"I heard Poppa and Mother speaking of Miss Barlow. Arguing, really," she'd explained when Hugh asked why she would think this woman was his mother. "Mother acted as if his affair with Nanny Catherine had been a farce. That she had agreed to raise you because she'd always wanted a child but had never married, but that Miss Barlow was in fact the true mother."

It was preposterous. Utterly impossible. "Whatever you overheard was wrong. You misinterpreted their words, I'm sure. My mother is Catherine Marsden."

"I'm sorry, I know this cannot be easy to hear," Eloisa said, looking as though she were indeed regretful. Clasping her hands and leaning forward in her chair, she'd looked at Hugh with a pity he didn't want.

"It's not difficult to hear, because I know it isn't true. You were ten years old when your mother died," Hugh said. "That means you were even younger than that when you overheard this argument. Children don't always hear correctly, and so much time has passed—"

"No. I know what I heard, Hugh. It's clear as daylight, even now. You didn't hear her, shouting about it, screaming that all would be lost. Mother was absolutely terrified that someone would learn about April Barlow. It is not something I would ever forget."

Eloisa held his stare, impressing that she held no doubt at all about what she was saying. Reluctantly, he indulged her.

"Why would she be terrified?"

"I don't entirely know, but I have learned that Miss Barlow is the daughter of a knight."

"Learned how? When?"

Eloisa stiffened her shoulders. "I can't tell you everything, for it will reveal things I need to keep secret. But if you find Miss Barlow, we might be able to ruin Bartholomew and Thomas."

Hunger for their undoing leaped like two wild flames in her eyes. It only made Hugh more curious. So, she wanted to ruin her brothers. After their actions six years ago, Hugh could understand why.

"Where will I find her?"

She pressed her lips thin. "That is why I've come. She is missing."

"How do you know this?"

Again, she retreated, shutters closing over her eagerness. "I can't say how."

"Then I can't help you." He was growing not just weary of this ridiculous claim, but angry. How dare she come here after so many years absent and tell him this? It was disrespectful, both to him and to his mother.

"Please," Eloisa pleaded, "just pay Sir Robert Barlow of Chatham Park a visit. You will see that I am in earnest. I can't go there myself. Coming here is enough of a risk. I'm not supposed to be in London—" She broke off, her voice warbling.

"Barty has ordered you to stay away, out of society. Forever?"

Eloisa hadn't answered him. She'd merely stood up, taken a pound note from her reticule, and tried to place it on Hugh's desk. He'd stopped her, telling her he didn't want her money. With a sob lodged in her throat, she'd nodded and fled his home.

Now, as the chaise exited a lane of mature poplars and came into view of a finely kept stone Tudor manor surrounded by snowy lawn, he wished he'd stood by his decision to dismiss Eloisa's request. Not only did he question the accuracy of her memories but her intentions too. The secrecy of how she'd learned of April Barlow's disappearance, the impetus of her mission to find her, and how in the world it could possibly ruin Barty and Thomas, made Hugh wonder if Eloisa was once again leaving him to take the fall for something.

And yet he could not walk away from such an accusation. He would prove that his mother *was* Catherine Marsden, and he would put any doubt about it to rest. For good.

Sir stayed with the chaise as Hugh presented himself at the front door. Coming to a large country manor like this put his mind back to the summer, when he had been summoned to Fournier Downs by the duchess to investigate a death. He wondered where Audrey was now. With the Season underway, she would likely be in London, chaperoning the duke's sister, Cassandra—if the young lady had returned from Sweden. Knowing the darkest, deepest secrets of the duke and duchess, and yet with no connection at all to their world, left him grasping. Several times, he had nearly sent a letter to Audrey, simply asking her if she was well. Several more times, he'd contemplated directing a hack to Curzon Street, just to catch a glimpse of Violet House. He'd never stooped to either temptation, thank God.

He supposed it didn't matter where she was. It would be best to put her out of his mind altogether.

Once Sir Robert had agreed to meet his unexpected caller, Hugh followed a footman into a drawing room. The room was cavern-like; dark and somber. Drapes shut out the bleak sunlight from several windows, except for one near a mahogany table. A man stood near that window, his arms crossed, his mouth turned down with a frown of impatience.

"You look remarkably like your father," the man said before Hugh could introduce himself. The footman would have given Hugh's name to the knight, and clearly Sir Robert knew him. He felt the floor tilt.

"You were acquainted with Viscount Neatham?" Hugh asked.

Sir Robert dropped his arms to his sides and strode toward a side table. He pulled the stopper from a decanter and poured two glasses.

"Many years ago. Though not under the best circumstances," he replied, his voice clipped. He came to Hugh and handed him a glass. "Why have you come?"

He gripped the cut crystal glass, his breathing off kilter. "I am looking for Miss April Barlow. I am told she is your daughter."

"She is," the knight answered. "Though I was assured that you would never learn of her."

A heaviness settled over Hugh's shoulders, like molten lead pouring down each arm and cooling rapidly. He placed the untouched drink on the nearest surface—a low table—and stared at the carpet below his feet.

"It is true then? She is my mother?"

Sir Robert quizzed him, the lines around his eyes deepening. "It is an unsavory story, one that I'd hoped would stay buried. But yes."

Heat swarmed, along with a stirring of nausea. Everything he'd believed, everything he'd known about his origins were now twisting into something unrecognizable.

"Why was I led to believe Catherine Marsden was my mother?"

She'd lied to him. All his life, until her dying breath, she'd *lied*.

Sir Robert sipped his drink with a detached air. "The spinster nanny, yes. I had heard that was the route Fitzgerald had taken. Apparently, he trusted her completely, and she longed for a child."

Fitzgerald. It was Hugh's middle name, and his father's Christian name. Sir Robert swept out his arm, indicating the couch and chairs near the hearth. Though he was restless, Hugh's legs felt numb and quivery. He gratefully lowered himself to the edge of a chair.

"Who has sent you here?" the knight—his *grandfather* —inquired.

Hugh looked into the older man's face again, seeing him anew. He tried to find some similarity about him. Some likeness or resemblance, but there was nothing. He'd been correct earlier; Hugh had always looked like his father. The same dark hair and somber brown eyes, the same chin and mouth.

"It doesn't matter who sent me." Eloisa was already uneasy to be in London; Hugh didn't know if he could trust Sir Robert with the details of her visit and inquiry. "I've come because it appears Miss Barlow is missing, and a concerned party would like to find her."

If the knight experienced any alarm or surprise at hearing his daughter was missing, he did not display it on his face. Nothing about him changed, other than a quick flare of his nostrils.

"Do you know where she is?" Hugh asked after a wasted moment spent waiting for the man to speak.

"Field Street Finishing School for Young Ladies, in Cheapside. She is headmistress there, and I highly doubt she is missing. She never leaves the place." He spread his hands. "I receive a letter once or twice a year. I suppose I should be grateful she thinks of me at all."

Hugh was accustomed to hearing the things people did not explicitly say. A bevy of disappointment and guilt bled through the knight's self-deprecating comment.

"The two of you are at odds?"

"Some would say we are too alike to get on well," Sir Robert replied. He was a straightforward man, not taking a moment to think or consider his replies. He didn't prevaricate or ponder. He was somber, serious, and he struck Hugh as cold and emotionless. Not mean, exactly, but aloof.

"She gave me to the viscount," Hugh presumed. At the man's nod, he asked, "Why?"

Again, the answer released rapidly from the tip of Sir Robert's tongue. "My daughter was selfish and impudent, and her mistakes cost this family greatly," he said. "She and the viscount conducted themselves poorly, rashly. I have never been one for London; I don't have the patience or tolerance for frippery or society, and I'd believed April to be the same. I was mistaken."

Hugh ran his hand through his hair, his temples beginning to ache. So, his father had conducted an affair, but not with the nanny. With a lady of the peerage. A young, unmarried lady. Hugh wanted that drink now, that was for damn sure.

He got up and went to the table where he'd left it, giving himself a moment to clear his mind and think of his next question. While standing there, sipping slowly, his eyes coasted across a painting positioned on the wall before him. It depicted two young women: one fair, the other slightly darker in complexion. The darker haired woman sat primly, hands folded in her lap. The other stood next to her chair, resting her hands on the dark-haired woman's shoulders.

They both looked an awful lot like their father. That same dry expression. The same strong jaw and somber, flat lips.

"April is seated," Sir Robert said, having noticed Hugh's interest. "The other is her younger sister."

Hugh's eyes perused the dark-haired woman. As he'd done with his grandfather, he waited to feel some pang of recognition, but all he could do was compare her to his memories of the woman who had raised him—his mother in truth, Catherine Marsden. Catherine had worn her graying curls up, but a few had always escaped her pins and she would end up tucking them behind her ear. Blue eyes, soft wrinkles, a kind smile. The fact that he had not resembled her in the least had never weighed on his mind; he'd simply taken after his father.

His eyes shifted to the other woman. His aunt. She was the prettier of the two, but not by much. A finer turned nose, doe-like lashes framing her eyes. Had the scandal of April bearing a child out of wedlock been made known, her younger sister would have also been ruined. Was that why April turned him over to the viscount? But that had been so long ago. With time, all things fade. His father had been dead for years. So had his mother—Catherine. What had been stopping April Barlow, or her father for that matter, from contacting him and telling him the truth?

"All this time, you've known about me and stayed away," Hugh said, a hollow sensation forming a pit in his stomach.

"It was what she wanted," the old man said. "It was the agreement."

"Agreement between whom?"

Sir Robert sealed his lips, a ready reply swallowed. "That is something you must ask her yourself."

Determined to find her and do just that, Hugh tossed back the rest of his drink and took his leave.

CHAPTER
FIVE

SUNDAY **A**FTERNOON

The windows and doors of Lady Reed's home had been thrown open to clear the sickly chemical smell, but Audrey could still trace the faintest remnants of the wretched odor as she was shown into the morning room the afternoon following the murder. Their footman had not taken Audrey's coat and gloves, advising she instead keep them to stave off the chilled air of the rooms.

As she crossed the ground floor lobby, a man in military uniform exited the room that the footman was leading Audrey toward. The man carried his shako hat under his arm, his jet hair neatly combed and pomaded, except for an artful curl across his brow. His full mouth and regal chin struck her as familiar, but it wasn't until his deep brown eyes rested upon her that she realized who he was. He looked incredibly like Hugh. Or rather, like the late Viscount Neatham.

Hugh's youngest half-sibling snapped his heels together and sketched a rigid bow. Audrey stopped.

"Good day. You are Lord Neatham's youngest brother, are you not?" she asked.

Surprise lit his expression before he schooled it into polite detachment again. "Yes, ma'am. Colonel Trenton, at your service."

Red veins streaked the whites of his eyes, and the waterlines were also irritated. Vestiges of weeping, she presumed.

"I am very sorry for what has happened," she said, then, because it would be far more direct to return Eloisa's ring to a family member rather than Lady Reed, Audrey reached into the pocket of her skirt.

"Here," she said, extending the small garnet ring. He peered at it, markedly confused. "I was present last evening when...well, I was the one who found your sister, and this was on the floor near her. I meant to give it to Lady Reed, or the Bow Street officers, but I'm afraid I became rather distracted."

It was an inane excuse. But she could not keep the ring, nor could she think of another way to return it. Thankfully, the colonel's interest did not rest on the strange explanation. He bowed again, this time a degree more intently.

"Forgive me, Your Grace, I did not know you were the duchess." He straightened, and then reached for the ring. He held it gingerly between thumb and forefinger. "This belonged to our mother. Thank you."

His voice sounded raspy, as one's voice often did when burdened by emotion. She imagined he'd been visiting with Lady Reed to discuss the events of the night before. The question of whether the marchioness had been honest with him about her earlier private meeting with Eloisa caused her to push the boundaries of their chance meeting.

When Colonel Trenton dipped into another bow, this one in parting, Audrey cut him off with a clearing of her throat.

"Do you have any idea why Lady Eloisa would have been at the soiree last night? It's my understanding that she was not expected to attend." It was the more polite way to say that the young woman had not been invited. Then again, she had not been on any guest list for many years, and for obvious reasons.

Colonel Trenton slipped the ring into a pocket of his uniform. "I'm afraid I couldn't say," he replied. "Lady Reed has expressed the same confusion."

He coughed and then grimaced. Guilt for badgering him warred with a longing for more information on what Eloisa and Lady Reed had been discussing before the murder. But she supposed a conference with the marchioness was her best bet for learning that.

"The duke and I express our condolences," she said, and then with a small bob of her head, allowed him to take his leave.

The footman, who had been standing aside, waiting while she spoke to the colonel, now entered the morning room to announce her.

A fire roared in the hearth, and a maid was tucking a thick quilted blanket around Lady Reed's feet. The marchioness reclined on a chaise, her stout body bundled as well as it would have been in an open sleigh, complete with mink muffler and matching mink-trimmed hat.

"Your Grace, what a surprise. Do come in. I apologize for the brisk air," Lady Reed began. Brisk was putting it somewhat mildly. It was no warmer indoors than out. "Did I hear you speaking with Colonel Trenton just now?"

"Yes, we met briefly," she replied, decided not to mention anything about the garnet ring.

"Poor young man. So despondent. So desperate to know

43

what his sister was doing here last evening," Lady Reed said with a long sigh. Audrey had the same burning question. But before she could echo it, the marchioness went on.

"He is to be married, you know. In less than a fortnight. Though now, I am not sure it would be proper to continue with such a ceremony. A wretched thing, too—the young lady is quite wealthy, I'm told. Oh, Ginny do bring tea," she called out to her maid. "This is unbearable! The windows have been open all night and morning in an attempt to fumigate the premises. I do not know how much longer I can stand it."

Lady Reed was far more talkative than she'd been the evening before when Audrey and Philip had approached her to thank her and take their leave. She'd been distracted then, and because of the garnet ring, Audrey now knew why.

"The smoke was quite peculiar," Audrey agreed, thinking of the haze that had seared their eyes and throats and nostrils. "Whatever the caustic chemical was, it was certainly employed to cause distraction and panic."

Which chemical it had been had also occupied a corner of her mind since the previous night. No flames had accompanied it, but certainly there were a number of chemical compounds that, when combined, could create such a reaction. Why, just a month or so ago, there had been a lecture at the Lyceum that touched on such things. A pair of chemists, Mr. and Mrs. Marcet, were to present on Mrs. Marcet's newly published chemistry book. Audrey had been desperate to attend, but Cassie had only just returned, and she had not wanted to leave her alone at Violet House.

However, Lord Thornton may have attended. If so, he could have an idea about which chemicals might have been used.

From under her blankets, Lady Reed's distressed expression pinned on Audrey. "Do you suggest that someone *planned* the events of last night?"

PENANCE FOR THE DEAD

Audrey sat a bit taller, surprised that the marchioness had not yet worked that out for herself. It seemed obvious.

"Of course," she said. "The smoke conveniently drove any witnesses from the ballroom. The murderer must have used the poor visibility to sneak up on Lady Eloisa."

Lady Reed's brow arched. "What a vivid imagination you have, Your Grace."

Her poorly masked condescension only inspired Audrey to get on with the reason for her visit.

"Last evening, you told Officer Tyne that you had not been aware of Lady Eloisa's presence in your home."

The marchioness scoffed. "That is correct. What of it?"

"I only wonder why you would withhold the truth." Lady Reed's relaxed position on the chaise stiffened. "It's been made known to me that you and Lady Eloisa met in another room of this home last night, before the unfortunate events."

"That is absurd," she hissed. "Where did you hear such nonsense?"

Her denial was not unexpected. Audrey shrugged and said, "Servants do love their gossip, my lady."

She fussed on the chaise, pulling at the blanket and huffing in exasperation. "Servants are also notoriously devious, Your Grace. I would think you would know that."

"Are you not acquainted with Lady Eloisa?" Audrey asked instead.

"Of course I am. She is—*was*—my relation by marriage."

Interest zipped up along the duchess's spine. "What is your connection?"

"Lila, Lady Neatham, is my niece," she explained. "My sister's daughter."

The maid reentered with a tea service, giving Audrey a few moments to sort this through. Lady Neatham, Bartholomew's wife, was Lady Reed's niece. Had she seen much of Eloisa in the past several years? Once the maid had poured for them and left, she asked that very question. The marchioness shook her head as she sipped her steaming oolong.

"No, I only encountered Eloisa before the scandalbroth that scattered that blackguard, Marsden, on an ill wind. Lila married the viscount shortly before the dreadful duel. Eloisa attended a few family parties. Afterward...nothing."

"Then why was she here?" Audrey asked. "Why try to speak to you, and during a soiree at that? It must have been some emergency."

Lady Reed's cup clattered onto the china saucer, the woman herself appearing rattled and perturbed. "How dare you call me a liar?"

Audrey bit her tongue, realizing she had been too heavy-handed, just as she had been last spring when she'd been hunting down evidence to clear Philip of murder charges. The urgency filling her to the brim to establish what truly had happened, and who was to blame, felt just the same as well. It was unforgivably rude to accuse Lady Reed of telling false-hoods, and yet Audrey knew that she had indeed lied. Rescinding the accusation would have no soothing effect. The damage had already been done. The least she could do now was leave here with answers.

"Very well, I will be frank." Audrey squared her shoulders and set her own teacup and saucer on the table. "I am the one who saw you, Lady Reed."

The marchioness gasped, her lips parting. "How could you have done?" Then, quieter, "We were alone."

"I am afraid you were not," Audrey replied, and not wanting to dive any deeper, continued, "Why tell Officer Tyne a falsehood?"

Lady Reed jutted her sharp chin. "This has to do with Eloisa's by-blow half-brother, doesn't it? The Bow Street officer you've been cavorting with." She let out a smirk when Audrey's eyes widened. "Oh yes, people speak of it, Your Grace. Do you think your fancy has gone unnoticed? He is missing now, or haven't you heard? Attacked the viscount before coming to my home—"

"You have no proof he was here." Audrey knew she sounded too eager to defend Hugh, and yet, she also could not curb her tongue. "Eloisa was asking you for something, and you denied her. What was it?"

The blankets fell away as Lady Reed stood, gaping at her. "You were spying on us?"

"I had the misfortune of happening upon you," she lied, though in some ways, it was true. It was a misfortune to have only heard a snippet of their conversation in the vision rather than all of it.

"She was asking dangerous questions, just as you are now, Your Grace," the marchioness said. It came as no great surprise when she then demanded that Audrey take her leave.

Calmly, Audrey stood, grateful she had not removed her outer trappings. It would save her time in departing. However now, after the confrontation, she was fully warm, her blood pumping hot.

"Whatever you are concealing, I ask that you reconsider. Lady Eloisa was murdered, and I mean to find out who killed her."

Lady Reed's teeth came on full display as she laughed haughtily. "My word, you've taken leave of your senses, Your Grace. Sullying yourself by playing at inspector! Whatever you think you know, it is wrong. Good day to you."

The marchioness sealed her lips and waited for Audrey to be gone. There was nothing more to be said. As she turned and left the sitting room, her shivers set back in. It wasn't the chilled air of the house. She'd been reckless. Within hours, all of London would know that she had barged into Lady Reed's home and acted like a madwoman.

A cold sweat erupted on her chest and back. She'd been foolish. Brazen. This would not go unnoticed or unremarked upon, that was for certain.

But Lady Reed had admitted to seeing Eloisa, and that Eloisa was asking dangerous questions. What could she have wanted from the marchioness? Her sister-in-law's aunt. A distant relation, at best.

Feeling more anxious and disturbed—and wholly unwise— than before, Audrey returned to the waiting carriage. Her driver Carrigan descended from the box, but before she could reach him, a small figure darted into her path. A skinny, knobby shouldered boy stopped and lifted the brim of his cap. Audrey's chest grew hot as her heartbeat doubled. The boy's cheeks appeared scrubbed, the cap, newly purchased. He wore trousers that reached all the way to his ankles now, and his boots, though not at a high polish, were solid without a single rip or hole.

"Sir?" she asked, disbelieving. "My word, you've grown at least an inch."

It wouldn't do to remark on his cleanliness. Or the fact that he didn't smell like a chamber pot.

"Got a message for you, duchess." Hugh's errand boy— though he was much more like his trusted streetwise assistant —was all business as he continued, "Tonight. Ten o'clock, sharp. Keep your bedchamber window cracked."

Audrey blinked, taken aback. "My bedchamber? Sir, what is this about? Have you seen Mr. Marsden?"

But the boy slipped away like spots of grease on water. He darted behind a pair of men in great coats and when Carrigan reached her side, Audrey could no longer see the boy.

"Are you unwell, Your Grace?" he asked. "Did that urchin bother you?"

"No, no, I am fine, Carrigan," she said, her pulse still racing.

As he handed her up into the carriage, she drew in a long breath, and cursed the hours still standing between now and ten o'clock.

Hugh was coming to see her.

CHAPTER
SIX

SATURDAY AFTERNOON

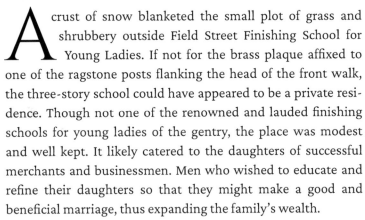

Acrust of snow blanketed the small plot of grass and shrubbery outside Field Street Finishing School for Young Ladies. If not for the brass plaque affixed to one of the ragstone posts flanking the head of the front walk, the three-story school could have appeared to be a private residence. Though not one of the renowned and lauded finishing schools for young ladies of the gentry, the place was modest and well kept. It likely catered to the daughters of successful merchants and businessmen. Men who wished to educate and refine their daughters so that they might make a good and beneficial marriage, thus expanding the family's wealth.

Hugh lingered at the ragstone post, trying like hell to convince himself that he wasn't hesitating. He'd returned from Chatham Park the evening before. After telling Basil he didn't wish to be disturbed, he'd shut himself inside his bedroom and tucked into a bottle of single malt. The whole distance back to

London, along the muddy and snowy roads, Hugh had been silent. Sir had known to leave off asking questions after Hugh met the first few with a clenched jaw and a shake of his head.

The scotch hadn't helped Hugh to understand why his birth mother had relinquished him to the viscount, to be raised by another woman. Nor had it educated him on why she'd stayed away, or why Eloisa was now coming forward with her discovery. Eloisa wanted to hurt Barty; she wanted vengeance. But how in hell was April Barlow going to manage that?

After a quick stop into Bow Street to see if there were any pressing matters, Hugh had given the address of the finishing school to a jarvey. It was on the outskirts of town, in residential working-class Cheapside. An icy wind had started to whip, and now Hugh held the brim of his hat to keep it from flying away. If he stood here much longer, he'd either freeze, or be confronted for skulking.

At the front door, he brought down the knocker and quelled the coiling of his stomach. Catherine Marsden, the woman who'd raised him, was dead. His coming here, seeking out April Barlow was not a betrayal. The lingering ache at the back of his skull reminded him of the scotch he'd indulged in the night before, while trying to convince himself of that.

The door opened, and he released his breath. Standing before him was a young woman, not very long out of school herself. She appeared stern with a pair of spectacles perched on her nose, and her dress was plain. That a man stood on the doorstep did not seem to faze her.

"Afternoon, sir. Please state your business," she said, not unkindly but with a certain lack of warmth.

He doffed his hat. "I'm looking for a woman by the name of April Barlow. I was told she is headmistress here."

"Your name, sir?"

"Principal Officer Hugh Marsden with Bow Street." At that,

the young woman's guarded expression brightened. She opened the door wider, considered another moment, and then stepped aside.

"You should come in."

It was only slightly warmer in the foyer when she shut the door behind him, and down the front corridor, a few young girls in braids and bows skittered quickly from view. The threadbare runner down the hall indicated a lack of funds to update the place, as did the utilitarian and uninspired décor; a few paintings on the walls showed dull landscapes and wizened faces of what he guessed were former headmistresses; either that or benefactresses.

"My name is Miss Carey, assistant headmistress at Field Street," she said, then, at the stifled sound of giggles down the corridor, she arched a brow. "Girls, back to your class."

The few girls spying from afar scattered.

"Forgive them, they are just as eager to find out where their headmistress has gone as I am. Mrs. Smith has sent you I presume? I had hoped someone would come to investigate, and here you are."

She clasped her hands before her and waited for him to speak. It took him a moment to comprehend what she'd said.

"Mrs. Smith," he repeated. "She said I would come?"

"Not specifically, but she mentioned she had a friend at Bow Street and would see what she could do," Miss Carey replied.

Understanding bowled through him. Mrs. Smith was surely Eloisa. "She did send word," he confirmed, "however, I'm still curious as to what would draw her here to begin with."

How had she known to come to this school? Eloisa had been ambiguous about how she'd come upon the name April Barlow again, after so many years.

Miss Carey, however, was not nearly as perplexed. With a small shrug, she replied, "She was interested in placing her child for our next term. When I informed her that the head-mistress had not been seen for two days, she was quite concerned."

Place her child? Eloisa had no child. It had been a ruse, then, to gain entry here and speak to Mrs. Barlow. Then, when she learned of the woman's disappearance, she'd come to Hugh for help.

"Have you reported Mrs. Barlow as missing?" he asked.

"No, not yet," she answered, adjusting her wire framed spectacles. A hint of regret played across her expression. "You see, Tuesday morning, I found her room empty, her suitcase gone. She left a note, saying she would be back as soon as possible, but...you must understand, this is highly unusual behavior for her. April has been here over two decades, and she's never so much as taken a holiday. To up and leave in the middle of the night is...well, it is utterly bizarre."

Sir Robert had mentioned something similar: that his daughter hardly ever left the school.

"Did her note say where she was going?"

"No, which dually concerned me."

While concerning to Miss Carey, it would not have been seen that way at Bow Street. No officer would have treated April's disappearance as anything worth investigating. She was a grown woman, she'd packed her things, and she'd left a note. There was nothing suspicious about any of it. But Hugh could see Miss Carey's distress and believed her that it was not normal behavior.

The timing was a bit dubious too. Just as Eloisa comes to London to search for her, the woman packs her things and hightails it from town? If he had to guess, he'd say April Barlow had known someone was coming to find her, and she didn't want to be found.

"Is there anyone she associates with?" he asked. "Any friends beyond this place? Husband? Family?"

He already knew she did not visit Chatham Park. But his throat cinched at the idea that she had married and had more children. It was a selfish and complicated thought, and one he knew could not be so, considering her name was still Barlow. The "Mrs." before it was surely for propriety's sake at the school. Miss Carey shook her head, confirming his deduction.

"If she has family, she doesn't speak of them. She is wholly devoted to this school and these girls."

The assistant headmistress assented to his request to view April's bedroom and office, and as Miss Carey had described most of the clothing in her clothespress was gone. While her bedroom was spare, the clutter filling her office told a story of purpose and passion. Books lined not only all available shelf space, but side tables, a worn chair, and they formed a tower in the corner. Paintings were so numerous each frame nudged a neighbor. Various maps hung on the wall too, not just of England but of South America, Africa, and France. And similar to Audrey's collection in her study at Violet House, glass paper-weights and trinkets lined the windows.

Hugh walked over to them, his thoughts sticking to the duchess. In his mind's eye, Audrey reached for the polished nautilus shell on her study windowsill. The one with the intricate scrimshaw carvings. He pictured her running her fingertips over the carvings, as if secret memories were pouring through her mind.

"If April had left for good, she would have taken most of her things," Miss Carey said, dispelling Hugh's image of Audrey. "I did not think Bow Street would consider her truly missing. However, her behavior is so unusual, it is worrisome."

He turned from the windowsill. "It does appear she will

return. I'm not certain there is anything to investigate." At her crestfallen expression, he added, "Not officially."

As his inspection skipped over April Barlow's desk, he noted an elegant frame. Enclosed in the gilt filigree, was a portrait. Drawing closer, he saw that it was a small oil painting of a young boy with a serious mien; dark locks of unruly hair, a pouting lower lip, two black eyes highlighted only by daubs of ochre. Hugh swallowed hard as he picked up the portrait.

"April had a son once," Miss Carey said softly.

"What happened to him?" Hugh asked, recalling how much he'd disliked sitting for the artist. The man had been impatient, and Hugh had shifted restlessly upon the stool too many times. The stuffy air had smelled of linseed oil, and he'd wanted to be outside, playing at adventures with Barty—if he would allow it.

But his father had asked Hugh to sit; said that it was to be a gift. And so, Hugh had done as asked. He had wondered once or twice where the finished portrait had gone. When larger portraits of Barty, Thomas, and Eloisa had been hung on the walls, and Hugh's portrait remained absent, he'd understood why. He'd always understood that he was not their equal. The viscount could not hang the portrait of his bastard son amongst those of his legitimate children. Yet still, he'd wondered where the little painting had gone.

"She doesn't like to speak of it, but it seems he died," Miss Carey answered.

Hugh returned the frame to the desk. "I see."

Why April would keep this portrait on her desk, to view every day, which would then require a concocted tale about a dead son, Hugh couldn't comprehend. Had she loved him after all? Had she given him up under duress? He had many questions, and if he wanted answers, he needed to find her.

They quit the study, and Miss Carey led him back toward the foyer, thanking him for coming and asking what else she might provide so that he could make sense of the head-mistress's disappearance. As they reached the bottom stair, a loud crash and clatter from a room down the front passageway startled them both. Raised voices followed, and the assistant headmistress adjusted her spectacles again. "Please allow me one moment, officer."

She hustled toward the commotion and wasn't more than a few strides away when a soft *"Pssst"* sounded from the upper landing. Hugh twisted to see an older student, a young lady of about fifteen, motioning for him to come to her. Curious, he took a few steps up.

"Mrs. Barlow had a visitor, sir," she said, not wasting a moment. She clearly didn't want to be caught speaking to him.

"Who?" he asked. "When?"

"A man. Monday night." She kept her voice low. "I don't know who he was, but they argued. Mrs. Barlow was quite vexed."

The disturbance downstairs was continuing with Miss Carey's raised voice, reprimanding someone.

"Why has Miss Carey said nothing to me about this?" he asked.

The girl's expression went a bit green. "She doesn't know. I'd be in trouble if I confessed to being out of bed at such a late hour."

He crossed his arms. "Out of bed, or out of the school?"

She looked at the stairs, sheepish. "When I returned, I heard voices from her office. The door was partly open."

"Did you see him?" When the young lady shook her head, Hugh asked, "Do you recall the man's name? Anything at all about him or what they were arguing over?"

Another shake of her head, and Hugh sighed, frustrated.

"But she called him 'my lord'," the girl added. "And he told Mrs. Barlow that if she didn't do as he asked, there would be 'unsavory consequences'. I stepped on a board then, and it let out a squeak, so I dashed off to my room."

This had been Monday night. By Tuesday morning, April Barlow had been gone. Miss Carey's voice became clearer as she came back into the corridor, reminding the young ladies to act more appropriately.

Hugh quickly thanked the young lady, who then darted off the landing, out of sight. He took the steps back down and met the assistant headmistress as she returned. She peered up the stairwell, as if aware that her guest had not stayed put.

"Is everything well?" he asked her. "That was quite a stir."

"Just some rambunctious pupils," she said.

She then thanked him again and anxiously escorted him out from the domain of young, impressionable ladies and onto the front walk. Once there, the snap of cold wind beat a little clarity into his muddled brain.

If April Barlow was the late Viscount Neatham's secret, and Eloisa believed finding her would bring ruin to Barty and Thomas, that left one shining suspect for who might have paid the headmistress a midnight visit, to warn her away.

Hugh pulled his collar higher and walked to the street, to hail a hackney. Though he'd vowed to never speak to him again, or set foot in his presence, there was no getting around it now. With April Barlow missing, and since Eloisa had skittishly refused to tell Hugh where she was staying while in town, there was only one place to go for answers.

He needed to pay a visit to his least favorite aristocrat: Lord Neatham.

CHAPTER
SEVEN

Sunday Evening

L ady Derby had not canceled her scheduled musicale, and Audrey was nearly certain that was to the utmost relief of all those who'd been planning to attend. If anyone assumed a woman's murder the evening before would dampen the ton's incessant need to mingle and keep up appearances, they would have been wide of the mark. If anything, the spectacle of Eloisa's death had spurred on a frantic need to socialize.

Even Audrey, with last year's scandal still clinging like bramble weed, had been called on several times that afternoon. The news that she and the duke had been among the first few people to find the body had made its way around town. After her return from Lady Reed's home, she'd hardly had enough time to dash off a letter to Lord Thornton to ask him about the Lyceum lecture she had missed featuring the married chemists, the Marcets, before their butler, Barton, had started fielding an influx of visitors.

With each one, Audrey expected to hear some comment on her behavior at Lady Reed's, but no one mentioned a thing. Perhaps it was too soon for the marchioness to have blabbed to her acquaintances about the duchess's revolting accusations. Or perhaps the woman would not breathe a word of it to anyone. That she had lied to Officer Tyne was true, and she wouldn't want to risk that coming out.

By dinner, Audrey's temples ached from the endless stream of visitors and their invariable questions about the murder. Those who had been on the snowy veranda with Audrey, Philip, and Cassie had all heard the scream too, but none of them had re-entered the ballroom. What had driven her to do so, they all wondered, some of them lauding her as heroic, and others as rash and unthinking. And isn't just so odd, many came around to saying, that it would be the Bow Street officer whom Audrey and the duke had so recently made an acquaintance with who stands accused?

It had been a trial to form polite replies, however she soon realized her responses were not truly being sought. What these callers wished to do was simply convey their suspicions and of course, take part of the commotion gripping the whole town. It was equally horrific and diverting, and by the time Audrey had dressed for dinner, her stomach roiled with distaste.

The only bright moment of the afternoon had been the arrival of a reply from Lord Thornton, in which he'd confirmed that he'd attended the Marcets' lecture. He also mentioned a curiously similar incident at the lecture; a smoke explosion experiment that had required a clearing of the lecture hall. He planned to inquire with Alexander and Jane Marcet themselves in their London home, and that he would see what he could discover about the smoke deployed at Lord and Lady Reed's soiree.

After sending a brief note of thanks, she went down to dinner, her head filled with ideas about potential connections to the smoke experiment at the lecture. Had it been the same kind of device used at the soiree?

She entered the dining room to find Philip, alone.

"Cassie has gone to Michael and Genie's for the night. Possibly for longer," he said by way of greeting.

Audrey stopped on her way to her seat and stared at him, dumbfounded. Cassie had deigned to sit in with a few of the day's callers, but eventually retreated to her room. She'd appeared pale and morose, and understandably so. But she had said nothing, nor sent word to Audrey that she was leaving Violet House.

"We will try to keep this hushed," he went on without meeting her eyes, preoccupied with placing his napkin in his lap. "I cannot fathom an excuse for her leaving that would not inflame the gossips right now. But she was adamant. I couldn't convince her to stay."

"Is she cross with us?" Audrey asked as she sat across from him at the table. To leave the home of her hosts was surely a snub.

"No," he said, finally looking up at her. He sighed. "She cannot stand the attention, that is all. This house will be over-run, as you can imagine. She is nervous. Lady Dutton's questions last night affected her."

It was small relief hearing the reason for her leaving, but it didn't settle Audrey. Far from it. Cassie couldn't escape whispers or questions just by switching roofs. Only time would quiet those wagging tongues.

"How was your outing this morning?" he asked quietly. With a pair of footmen standing in the corners of the dining room, nothing could be said specifically. She did not understand why he'd even bothered to ask.

"Brief," Audrey replied. Then, "I saw Colonel Trenton there."

Philip frowned into his glass of wine. "He must be in town for the military review. You remember we are attending on Wednesday with Michael and Genie?"

As Audrey spread her napkin over her lap, she groaned audibly at the reminder of their upcoming outing to the military review in Hyde Park.

"I know you don't enjoy them," Philip said in an attempt to stave off her usual complaint.

"But Michael looks forward to them, yes," she sighed. Philip's brother, having been commissioned into the Royal Army during the war in France, adored the reviews. Though he was no longer commissioned, they allowed him to reminisce, and the last few they had all attended together, he'd been a fount of commentary during the drills and reenactments.

"The toll they take on the park landscape is absurd," Philip said with a snort of derision. "The troops and their horses leave it a terrific mess."

Leave it to Philip to consider the affect the reviews had on the flora and fauna of a place. She grinned and sipped her wine. This was the first she had seen her husband since that morning, and though she was a little envious that he had not had to endure the social calls as she had, she also couldn't be overly vexed about it. Or about anything else, for that matter.

Meeting with Sir and hearing his brief message outside Lady Reed's home had left her tingling with anticipation all day. It had been the only thing pulling her through the long afternoon.

Their soup arrived, and she and Philip ate in relative quiet for a short while. Audrey's thoughts were anything but quiet, though. Sir's instruction to keep her bedroom window open led her to think that someone might attempt to enter through it. Would it be Sir with some message from Hugh? Or Hugh himself? Ten o'clock wasn't terribly late. In fact, it might be too early. She would have to dismiss Greer sooner than usual and ask not to be disturbed. The undercurrent of eagerness couldn't be denied. Her skin practically itched with it.

"I met with an old friend today."

Audrey's ears had grown accustomed to the silence of the room while she'd picked at her venison pie, too nervous to eat. Philip's voice sounded like the crack of a gunshot. She looked up at him.

"An old friend?" she echoed.

He placed his utensils down and sat back, as if finished with his pie as well. He cleared his throat. "Yes, someone I had not thought to see again." The timbre of his voice was much softer than usual. Apprehensive, almost.

While waiting for him to name the person he'd been reunited with, the footmen stepped forward to clear their plates. With much practiced precision, the door to the room opened and another footman emerged with bowls of trifle. Guiltily, Audrey knew that she would not be able to take more than a single bite. Mrs. Comstock had worked all day to provide this meal, and would be receiving it back, as if it was not appreciated.

"Can you please have mine sent to my room?" she asked of the footman before he could place it before her. He whisked it away, and Audrey thought to give it to Sir, should the boy be the one to arrive.

"Are you not well?" Philip asked.

"Just a bit tired," she said lamely. The tedious excuse would have to do. Confessing she might be receiving a caller that night via her bedroom window was out of the question. Especially if it was a man wanted by the authorities.

"This friend," she said to redirect the conversation, "who is it?"

Philip was not one to shrink away from a question; his mind worked in such a way that he didn't require time to ponder or consider a reply carefully. His ability to converse, to cut with dry wit, or impress with an intelligent response were among his greatest attributes. And yet, he now hesitated. It was as if he'd changed his mind and didn't wish to speak of this friend that he himself had just brought up.

"A Cambridge mate," he said after a moment, then pushed back his chair to stand, adding, "who I have agreed to meet tonight at Brooks's. I may be very late."

With a quick glimpse at the mantelpiece clock, she tried not to show her delight. What luck! Very late likely meant early morning, especially if he hadn't seen this friend in some time.

"Is Carrigan driving you?" she asked.

"Unless you are attending the musicale?" Philip pinned her with a knowing look. One of his other great attributes was having a keen memory and caring enough to keep track of her planned schedule. Evidently, he also presumed that she'd sent her regrets earlier in the day, which she had.

"I am curling up in bed after a long bath," she said, and it wasn't a complete lie.

He departed, and Audrey swiftly made her way to her room. There were still two hours yet until the arranged time, so she did indeed bathe and have Greer towel and dry her hair.

"Just a braid tonight," she told her maid, not wishing for Sir or Hugh, depending on who arrived, to see her in curling papers.

Greer plaited Audrey's thick blonde hair and draped it over her shoulder. Then, at Audrey's urging, she took her leave for the night.

She paced as the designated hour grew close. The trifle had

been sent to her room, as requested, but just looking at it on the table near her chaise made her stomach turn. Though it was freezing outside and still windy, she opened the sash a few inches and peered into the darkened lawn below. Only her reflection in the glass showed.

Where was he? The police had been hunting him all day. He couldn't have gone back to Bedford Street or to Bow Street, though perhaps he'd been hiding at Lord Thornton's home on St. James's Square after all. Otherwise, he might have been out in this wretched weather.

Twisting her fingers together, she traveled the carpet's circumference several times, eyes jumping to the window on every turn. The room was cold after a quarter hour, the fire in the grate not enough to battle the March air gusting inside. When her fingers started to prickle from the chill, she gave in and went to her boudoir, where her robe hung. With a start, she realized she'd been so preoccupied that she'd been pacing in nothing but her nightdress and stockings. Quickly, she draped herself in a sapphire blue, embroidered India silk robe and tied the belt with a sigh of relief.

Audrey left the boudoir—and a pair of arms grabbed her from behind. Before she could shout, a coarse hand clamped down over her mouth. She was tugged back, against a solid chest and stomach. A muscled arm trapped her in place as she struggled.

"Easy, duchess," a voice whispered into her ear. "It's only me."

CHAPTER
EIGHT

Saturday Evening

～

Far from the center of London, Kensington Square had always given Hugh the impression of a sleepy, countryside corner. A few miles west from here, past Kensington Palace, Hyde Park, and Mayfair, lay Covent Garden and Bow Street, where he had spent the last years burying the many memories that he'd formed here, around the garden square enclosed by fashionable homes.

Neatham House looked no different than it had when Hugh had been living there. But he couldn't fool himself into believing the soul of the place hadn't mutated into something disappointing and foreign. And not just because Barty had taken the helm here after their father's death.

One lie often led to a second, and then a third, and now Hugh questioned where the lies would end in regard to April Barlow. If Eloisa knew about the woman, so might Barty. It seemed out of character for him to have visited the Field Street school himself, but if Barty wanted to ensure total privacy, he could not have sent a man to relay his message.

Hugh climbed the three whitewashed steps to Neatham House's front entrance and with a knot in his stomach, brought the pineapple-shaped brass knocker down thrice. The pineapple was the symbol of hospitality, and so it adorned many of the more gracious homes in town. He scoffed at it here, however, knowing the viscount's hospitality would not extend to his exiled half-brother.

The door opened, revealing a footman Hugh did not recognize.

"Officer Hugh Marsden of Bow Street to see his lordship."

The servant gave him a once over before advising him to stay put. He then closed the door in his face. The name of his employer's past enemy must have been made known to all and sundry at Neatham House. Hugh darkened the doorstep for a full ten minutes—just long enough for him to think the footman did not plan to return—before the door opened again.

"His lordship will see you in his study."

Hugh doffed his hat as he entered the entrance lobby. The décor had changed some, though the oil portrait of their father, Fitzgerald Humphrey, still hung on the same wall at the stair-case landing.

"This way," the footman said, starting up the stairs.

Hugh knew where the study was—he'd spent endless hours in it with the late viscount—but followed the servant for propriety's sake. He hadn't come here to cause trouble or a scene. This was an investigation. He had questions, and Barty likely had answers.

When the footman showed Hugh into the study, he took a deep breath, expecting the pleasant scents of pipe tobacco and cedar wood. But of course, those scents were not present. They were mere memories, attached to his long dead father. Instead, he found a slightly older and heavier version of Bartholomew than he'd been six years ago. He stood next to his desk, waiting for Hugh to enter. Though only four months older than Hugh, he had the soft paunch and chin that so many lords developed, along with thinning hair. Their father's hair had been full and thick to the end; Barty had always favored his mother's looks.

"You are not welcome here, Marsden," was the greeting he received.

The footman closed the door behind him, and Hugh stepped forward, toward the same cherrywood desk that had been their father's.

"Then I will make my visit as brief as possible." He remained standing, his eyes taking in his brother's face. Still the same old Barty, wearing the expression of a man who'd just cracked open a rotten soft-boiled egg.

"Do that," Barty said. "Lila will be displeased if she gets wind that you are here."

The viscountess might have cared for Hugh even less than Barty did. Instead of dying in the duel, as planned, he'd had the audacity to shoot her husband and cripple him.

"You paid a call on Field Street Finishing School earlier this week, did you not?" Hugh asked.

Barty walked around his desk, his face screwed up into a scowl. "No, I did not. Why the devil would I call on a finishing school?"

"To speak to Miss April Barlow," Hugh answered.

"I don't know anyone by that name."

Hugh's theory quickly began to dissipate. He knew Barty's expression when he was lying; he adopted a blasé arched brow and shrugged more than was necessary. But now, as he continued to sneer at Hugh, he only appeared aggravated.

"Nearly six years without seeing you and the first thing you do is ask me insipid questions. My God, Bow Street truly was desperate to take you on." Barty snorted mean laughter and plopped into the chair behind his desk. He laced his fingers over his stomach and stared at Hugh. "Well? Is that all?"

The mysterious lord the pupil at Field Street had heard in April's office the other night had not been Barty, then. As simple as the theory would have made things had it panned out, Hugh had to admit it had been too convenient. Too easy.

"No," he went on, letting the viscount's insult slide past. "Are you aware Eloisa is in town?"

The expression of arrogant disdain slipped. It seemed he still could not discipline himself against revealing his thoughts and feelings so openly. He was anything but shrewd, and without having to even speak, he gave his answer: Barty had not been wise to Eloisa's presence in London.

"What is the little fool doing here?" he asked.

"Not in your interest for her to visit, is it?" Hugh replied, his blood beginning to simmer as he looked at Barty, ensconced in their father's old, quilted leather chair. "Eloisa has come, and you are worried she will be seen. Why is that I wonder?"

The viscount did not know the name April Barlow, but he did have something to fear when it came to his sister. It could have just been damage to his reputation by proxy; Eloisa's presence, if made known, would drag up old demons and fodder for the gossips. But Barty's sharpened eyes, sealed lips, and the panicked flare of his nostrils hinted toward something more considerable.

"There was a baby," Hugh said, speculating, his stomach cramping in protest. "You don't want anyone learning of it."

The panic on his half-brother's face subsided, to be replaced by a suddenly cautious expression.

"Of course, I don't want anyone *learning* of it," Barty replied waspishly. "Five, fifteen, fifty—it doesn't matter how many years pass, the truth will always be a cancer on this family."

"You are wrong. The cancer is not the truth. It is the hushed-up secret you sold your soul to protect." Hugh clenched his jaw, knowing his patience was thinning and that it could prove disastrous.

"I did what needed to be done to protect my family."

That he did not consider Hugh family was no new stab of insult; he'd never felt a brotherly connection to Barty, nor to Thomas. Eloisa had always been aloof, urged by the late viscountess to keep her distance from the unfortunate family ward.

"You were merely protecting yourself," Hugh scoffed. "But continue to fool yourself if it helps you sleep at night."

Barty stood from his chair. Taller and broader in the shoulder, perhaps he wanted to intimidate Hugh into backing down. But by standing, all he succeeded at was showcasing the arm that had been shattered in the duel. The left arm seemed to have withered; the muscles, useless as they were, unable to develop as the right had over the last several years. The left simply hung there, no better than a dead appendage.

"You have never respected your place in this household, Marsden. You always thought you were something more, something better."

"I think the problem, brother, is that *you* think I am. For whatever reason, despite your title and birth right, you feel inferior."

"Inferior? To you?" Barty barked laughter, but the false note of it made Hugh's back teeth ache. "You are delusional, Marsden."

There was no reasoning with Barty. He'd concocted a rivalry between them that apparently still consumed him. It didn't matter. Hugh had not come here to comb over the past.

"April Barlow. Headmistress at Field Street Finishing School for Young Ladies. Do you or do you not know her?"

He'd raised his voice, attempting to get back to the point of his visit.

"I have already answered your question and it has not changed. What does she have to do with Eloisa?"

Informing Barty on anything more could jeopardize the tempting possibility of April Barlow somehow bringing ruination down upon his lofty head. Not answering his question would also leave him frustratingly peeved. Hugh grinned and turned toward the door.

"Good day, my lord. Forgive my insipid questions."

"Is this about the baby?" Barty rushed to ask. "Because it died, as it should have."

The cruel sentiment stopped Hugh in his tracks. It seemed to suck the very air out of the room. He slowly turned back toward Barty, who gave an insouciant sniff. "Better still if Eloisa had gone with it, but she always did wiggle out of a hard spot, didn't she?"

The whistling sound of wind, funneling down a narrow passageway filled Hugh's ears and head, and the next thing he knew, his control snapped. He shoved a chair aside and leaped across the desk, scattering papers and an ink pot. He and Barty went down in a tangle of thrashing arms and legs, with Hugh's knuckles connecting decisively with the viscount's smug face. Barty's howling drew company, and within seconds, a pair of footmen were tearing at Hugh's arms and pulling him off the viscount.

"Get that ingrate out of my house!" Barty screamed. "Call for the police! I will not be treated thus!"

"You!" The viscountess's shriek reached Hugh's ears. She filled the doorframe as the footmen dragged Hugh toward it. "How dare you enter this home and attack my husband? You will pay for this!"

Lila Neatham glared at Hugh with the same loathing she'd

shown him years ago. He paid her no attention as he wrenched his arms from the footmen's iron-like grips.

"I will go, and with pleasure," he told them, not sparing his half-brother or the viscountess another glance or word. He took the stairs to the entrance lobby, and then stalked out the front door. He was on the pavements when he felt the throb of his lip; he tasted blood. Barty had gotten in a punch then.

Passersby on Kensington Square slid from Hugh's path, alarmed by the bloodied man in a fit of temper. Regret swirled in his gut. His anger had started stewing before even entering Neatham House, and the comment about Eloisa being better off dying alongside her child had been his breaking point. His vile brother had claimed the high ground. Hell, Hugh had practically handed it to him. To make things worse, he was leaving no wiser about April Barlow.

Hugh flagged a passing hackney driver. He was finished. If Eloisa wanted to find Miss Barlow, then she was welcome to it. But he was done hunting the woman down. In less than a few days, he'd upended nearly six years' worth of progress in burying the warped muddle of his past.

The hired cab pulled to the curb, but then Hugh waved the driver on, changing his mind. He needed to move, and a mile down the Knightsbridge turnpike should do it. There would be a tavern along the way to stop in and drown his frustration. There was no one waiting on him at home anyhow.

"Bloody terrific," he grumbled, and kept walking.

CHAPTER
NINE

Sunday Evening

The arm that had snaked around Audrey from behind tensed, the gloved palm over her mouth stifling her instinct to scream. She went still. Then, pleasure broke through her, flooding her with warmth and chasing away any fear. It was Hugh's hand, Hugh's arm, no random intruder. He lowered his palm from her mouth, and as she spun to face him, she simultaneously threw her arms around him.

He stiffened only a moment before indecision melted away. His arms came around her again and he returned the embrace, holding her close with more might, more hunger, than she'd expected. For the span of several breaths, Hugh's lips coasted against her forehead. As she felt his lips kiss her brow, Audrey pulled back with a quick gasp of surprise.

"Where have you been?" she asked, noting his grime-smudged cheeks. A welt and a fresh bruise darkened under one eye. "You're hurt."

He shook his head. "I'm not hurt."

Wind whistled through the gap in the open window, and she left Hugh's hold to shut the sash and draw the drapery. The plane tree outside and its broad, stretching branches had provided him access to the narrow ledge of her window embrasure.

She turned back to him. "How did you know which room was mine?"

He had never been in here before. That he stood within her private bedchamber set off another uneasy spark under her skin.

Hugh grinned wryly. "Sir. And he distracted the two foot patrols on Curzon Street to give me time to climb up."

Of course there were patrolmen watching Violet House; she should have thought of it before. Bow Street knew of Hugh's connection to her. They might have anticipated his coming here. And she needn't have asked how Hugh had known which window was hers. Sir was adept and clever and had likely spied on Violet House's many upstairs windows until he knew for certain which set of rooms belonged to her. Hugh was no less adept or clever; he'd come through her window as stealthily as a burglar. Thought it had been an awful risk.

The crackling of the fire filled the silence for a moment. Then, Hugh stepped toward her, his eyes grave and pleading. "I didn't kill her."

"I know you didn't."

"I would never have hurt her. She's my sister," he added, as if he hadn't heard Audrey's reply.

She met him where he stood on the carpet and grasped his arms. "You don't need to convince me, Hugh. I *know* you didn't harm her."

He held her gaze, his eyes roving over her face, her dressing gown. Down to the tips of her stockinged toes. "I will leave if you don't want me here. I know this is deplorable—"

"Stop." He did as she commanded and sealed his lips. She released him, overwhelmed by how intensely she wanted him to wrap her into another embrace. A bit frightened by it too. "You will stay. Of course, you will stay."

Hugh nicked off his hat and scrubbed a hand through his disheveled dark hair. His rumpled clothing and lack of a neckcloth would have surely made his valet weep; dirt, or perhaps grease, spotted his collar and waistcoat, and his hands and nails were also streaked with grime. Good lord, he needed a bath.

"Where have you been?" she asked again. He would not have become this dirty if he'd been hiding in Lord Thornton's home on St. James's Square.

"Whitechapel mostly. Wherever I could stick to the shadows." He tossed his hat onto the blue silk chaise, where she often liked to read, and then shed his coat. With his hands on his hips, he twisted back to look at her. "You found her. At the soiree, the newssheets reported that you and the duke found her."

She had spent the whole day entertaining curious and calculating minds by relaying the story of how she and Philip came to discover the poor woman's body. But it was only now that she felt the same pangs of shock and distress, of cold disbelief, that had gripped her the evening before, in those terrible moments. Something about Hugh Marsden caused the protective walls Audrey tended to stand behind to disappear. For reasons she couldn't quite determine, she was as readily honest with him as she was guarded with mostly everyone else.

Renewed shivers wracked her body, and Audrey wrapped her arms around herself. "Yes. I found her. The duke wasn't very far behind me."

"I read she was stabbed. In the back?"

Audrey nodded, the motion strained by tensing muscles along her spine and neck. The room was still chilled from having the window sash open for nearly half an hour. A few strides brought her before the fire. With any hope, the heat of the flames would stop the shivers jittering through her.

"I took her ring," she admitted. "I wanted to see what it might reveal."

"And?"

Quickly, she divulged to Hugh what the ring had shown her, and then, of her ill-fated visit to the marchioness that morning.

"She didn't want Tyne to know she'd seen Eloisa," Hugh said, having crossed the bedroom to stand near the fire too. "To avoid having to confess the reason for Eloisa's visit, no doubt."

Lines of concentration cut into his brow as Hugh peered into the fire, as though mulling something over. The firelight brought his bruised eye and a split bottom lip into better view. Audrey closed her hands into fists to stop herself from reaching a gentle finger to his injury.

"I returned the ring to Colonel Trenton," she said, not wanting any stretch of silence to settle over them. It would be safer to remain occupied, to ignore that they were alone, in her bedchamber.

"Trenton?" he echoed, snapping the name with harsh surprise. He peered at her, the firelight creating a devilish shadow to arch above his brow. "When did you see him?"

"At Lady Reed's," she replied, curious as to his alarm. "He was leaving as I was arriving."

Audrey sealed her lips against describing his red-rimmed eyes and hoarse voice; conveying the details of Hugh's younger half-brother's grief would have smacked of gossip. The hardening lines of his jaw, and his newly dull and distant glare into the flames, hinted that he did not care to know anyway.

"I said the ring was on the floor near her..." She bit back the word 'body' and kept silent. "You aren't on good terms with him then, I take it."

He rolled his head, stretching the muscles along his neck, and then squinted into the fire as if eyeballing a particularly disgusting object. "No. I have not spoken to him in six years, and nor do I wish to."

Colonel Trenton had been perfectly polite to Audrey, but then, she was a duchess, not his accused half-brother. She could not judge or censure Hugh for his feelings. Rather, she trusted them. She combed back over the memory of her meeting with his half-brother. His grief-stricken appearance still pulled at her heartstrings.

"He is betrothed," Audrey said, recalling what Lady Reed had imparted.

"I do not care."

Very well then. She would seal her lips about Colonel Trenton.

"Eloisa came to see me," Hugh went on. "Thursday afternoon."

Audrey's stomach dropped. Hugh had known Eloisa was in London again, and she had gone to him? And just days before she'd died. The uneasy twist of her stomach at the revelation perplexed her, but she said nothing and allowed him to explain.

Hugh started at the beginning, with Eloisa's odd request to find the woman named April Barlow and her theory that she was, in fact, Hugh's birth mother. Audrey held her astonishment and questions in check as he continued, telling of his visit to Chatham Park, the secrets Sir Robert had revealed about the former viscount and his daughter, who was now apparently missing. It had been nearly one week since she was last seen by her students and the Field Street school assistant headmistress,

Miss Carey. When Hugh described the oil portrait that he'd found on Miss Barlow's desk at the school, and his own memories of sitting for that painting, Audrey could no longer hold back her amazement.

"Hugh..." But she found she didn't know what more to say. These revelations, piling upon him over the last few days, and now, the murder of his sister and the accusations against him, would be enough to cow anyone.

But he wasn't just anyone. He was Principal Officer Hugh Marsden. And he had come to her for help. If she knew him at all—and she believed she did—he did not want to wallow in the knowledge that he'd been deceived. That the woman who had raised him was not his mother in truth. No, Hugh would want to solve the problem at hand—Eloisa's murder.

"Lady Reed said Eloisa was asking dangerous questions at the soiree," Audrey said, changing course. "She didn't say what those questions were, but when I held the ring, I saw Lady Reed adamantly refusing her, telling her no."

Hugh turned from the hearth and paced toward the four-poster bed. "Eloisa was under the impression that the truth about April Barlow would ruin Barty. That it would destroy him. Thomas, too."

"How so?" Even with Miss Barlow as his birth mother, Hugh would still be illegitimate. She might very well be the daughter of a knight, but that would not absolve him of being born out of wedlock. What was it about April Barlow that Eloisa had wanted to reveal?

"I'm not sure," Hugh said with a long sigh. But there was also a strange inflection on his tone. She suspected that he was withholding something from her.

Hugh wandered around the bedstead, toward the dish of trifle that had been delivered to her room, as requested.

"If Eloisa was aware that Miss Barlow was your mother," Audrey began, turning to pace toward the bed, "and if her intention was to destroy Viscount Neatham, as you say...then perhaps the killer's intention was to stop her from succeeding."

She heard the veiled accusation as soon as the words left her tongue, and her cheeks instantly flushed. Hugh, however, only tapped his finger against the glass dish of trifle, as if in thought. "Barty would not kill his own sister."

"I'm sorry, I shouldn't have—"

"Don't apologize. You've only said what my mind has already considered. Speak your thoughts, Audrey—I came to you for help." He looked at her from across the expanse of the bed. Her flush traveled from her cheeks, down her throat, to her chest. Not from embarrassment, but from having him here, in this place that was her private sanctuary.

"I want to be able to help you. I *will* help you," she said. It was a promise. A vow. Her throat constricted, but she cleared it with a small cough. "Is there anyone else helping you?"

He averted his eyes. "Just Sir."

She couldn't believe it. "Surely Lord Thornton? Your valet? Sir Gabriel Poston?" The chief magistrate was one of Hugh's staunchest supporters.

He shook his head. "Thornton and Basil are the first people the other officers will predict I've turned to, and Sir Gabriel is a Bow Street man through and through; I can't go to him until I've proof in my hands." He raised an open palm and closed his fingers, as if clutching at imaginary evidence. "Sir will do what he can, but my association with him is well known, especially at Bow Street."

"I see. Is there no one else?" She fidgeted with the embroidered collar of her banyan. She wondered if there was a woman, or a companion of some kind. He was a handsome man, and at his age, shouldn't he have certain...needs? In the past, her mind had consistently rejected those thoughts whenever they'd sneaked in, but now, she couldn't be so selfish. Another ally of any kind would be beneficial to him.

But he shook his head again. "I can count those I trust completely on one hand."

"I am one of them?"

"I wouldn't be here if you weren't."

She bit back a pleased grin. But then, it broke through. Feeling a little giddy, she asked, "Am I the thumb?"

He huffed laughter. "You are whichever finger you find least offensive." He motioned toward the untouched trifle. "Are you planning to eat that?"

"No. Oh! You must be famished." Audrey started around the bed, toward the bedroom door. She hadn't considered that he might be hungry after two days on the run. "I'll fetch some tea and dinner."

"That isn't necessary. I didn't come here to put you out."

"If you're going to be eluding the police, you'll need sustenance," she replied, then paused to gesture toward the boudoir. "You can wash up in there. There's soap and water."

He rubbed the back of his neck as he craned his head toward the entrance to the boudoir. "The duke?"

Her heart gave a stronger than normal thump. "Out. Probably until morning."

With a prickle of awareness, she realized Hugh could rest here the night. He must have concluded the same thing, for he seemed to take a much longer breath than usual. The muscles along his jaw ticked.

"You're safe here," she said softly. "I'll be right back. And then you can tell me why you went to Neatham House. The newssheets said you attacked the viscount."

And the bruises at his eye and on his chin appeared to be the consequences of it.

"Of course, they would say that. It was a mistake to go there." Hugh picked up the trifle and speared it with a spoon. "I think it might be what got Eloisa killed."

TEN

The boudoir was a cloud of silk and satin, of white muslin and thin linen and all manner of lush, feminine possessions. Shedding his waistcoat and shirt, Hugh approached the ironstone pitcher and bowl on a stand with the same wary hesitance a doe might possess upon entering an open field. This was no place he'd ever anticipated being. The scent of camellia and jasmine bath oils still lingered, and he could not resist the delectable image of Audrey submerged in the clawfoot copper tub.

Quickly, he picked up the delicate round of milled French soap on a dish next to the basin and lathered a cloth. She would not take long to gather tea and a plate of food in the kitchen and return. She was right; he was famished. He'd hunkered down in a corridor in Whitechapel most of the day, watching the secret location of Thornton's community clinic. As it was a Sunday, he'd anticipated his friend to turn out for his weekly hours there. But he hadn't come. Out searching for Hugh, no doubt.

The evening before, he'd been nursing his swollen and bruised eye with a cold compress and a stiff whisky when Sir had come storming inside the house, shouting. Word on the street was that a lady had been killed at a fancy party in Mayfair and the Runners were coming—for Hugh. He'd barely had time to throw on his coat and hat and stuff some money into his pockets before Basil shunted him out the back door.

Sir led him to a warehouse to lay low and had then left to scout out the ordeal. He'd returned with the news Hugh had already begun to suspect: the woman was Eloisa. And Hugh was wanted in connection.

It was preposterous, of course, but not if viewed at as an outsider. Hugh, who'd been accused of ruining her years ago, and who had just gone a decent round of fisticuffs with Lord Neatham in his study, would certainly be the most likely suspect. And since he left Neatham House shortly before Eloisa's murder, the timing supported the accusations against him. As did his lack of an alibi. He hadn't gone back to Bedford Street via hired hack right after the altercation. Instead, he'd cooled off by walking the few miles home and taking his time to do it. He hadn't even stopped into a tavern for a pint, which would have given him an alibi. He'd spent the time alone, pondering the disastrous visit to his half-brother, the information he'd gleaned from his tour of the finishing school, and the unsettlingly swift way his past had caught up and closed around him like a vise since Eloisa's visit.

And now, she was dead. It wasn't exactly loss or sadness that he felt; perhaps that would come later. What he felt instead were stabs of regret and anger and frustration. They burned incessantly in his chest. If only Eloisa had been more forthcoming with her purpose here, her plans, then perhaps Hugh would have a suspect to corner and investigate. Not an official Bow Street-endorsed investigation, no, but one that was vital. The most vital he'd ever undertaken. The only person he could think of who stood something to gain from her death was Barty—just as Audrey had deduced. But not only would he never kill his own sister, he also had not been at the ball. Instead, he'd been busy reporting Hugh's attack on him to Bow Street. His alibi was unassailable.

He scrubbed the dirt and sweat from his arms, chest, and neck and dressed, now smelling faintly of lavender. It was the first bit of lightness he'd felt in days. Ever since Eloisa stepped into his study and thrown his world into a tailspin.

The door to the main bedchamber opened. Hugh waited, still not entirely trusting that the duke would not return from his club or the maid, Greer, would not pop in for one last task before turning in for the night.

"Hugh?" It was Audrey's tremulous voice. He exhaled.

"I'm here," he replied, stepping from the boudoir. The sight of her in her robe, though it covered her thoroughly from neck to ankle, still made him want to groan. As did the single braid, tied off with a ribbon and draped over her shoulder. She appeared soft and slumberous as she set the tray upon the chaise. He swallowed the groan and focused on his cuffs, then his placket and high collar. He'd left off the neckcloth.

"You smell much better," she commented as he approached the chaise.

"This room is a far cry from malodorous warrens of Whitechapel," he said, sniffing his sleeve. It wasn't all that offensive—yet. Give it another day and he'd be ripe.

She poured them tea, and when she lowered herself to the edge of the chaise, clasping her teacup with both palms, Hugh took the nearby chair. Best to keep at least a little distance.

"Did Lord Neatham give you that bruise?" she asked, sipping the brew.

"Either him or his footman when he pulled me off Barty," Hugh replied. "It was all a little hectic."

The black tea loosened the bunched muscles along his shoulders and spine. He'd been tensed all day, waiting for

Thornton to show, waiting for nightfall so he could see Audrey. Waiting to be found and arrested.

"Why did you go there?" she asked. "Why attack him?"

"I didn't attack him," he retorted, though much too aggressively. Defensively. He softened his voice as he set the small cup onto its saucer. "The visit was civil enough, at least at first."

He downed the rest of his tea, hoping it would warm his insides. The weather had chilled him to the bone all day, and even here, in this warm, posh room, the cold wouldn't abate.

Briefly, Hugh informed her of his visit and the pertinent details of what they'd discussed. He omitted the talk of Eloisa's baby. It turned his stomach, and surely would Audrey's too. Besides, it wasn't relevant to the murder case.

"He hadn't known she was in town?" Audrey asked afterward.

"And he hadn't been pleased to hear it." Hugh's blood had started to boil as he'd sat across from Barty in the study, over the glossy expanse of the viscount's desk, listening to his half-brother rattling off all the reasons why Eloisa's return would be disastrous if made public. Disastrous for *Barty*, that was.

"He knew nothing of April Barlow?" Audrey asked, drawing him back into the bedchamber and away from the memory of Neatham House. Snug and cozy, the corners of her room were dark with shadows where the lamplight didn't reach.

She poured more tea into his cup, and he sipped it more genteelly this time. Less like a rabid dog with a bottomless hunger.

"Nothing," he confirmed. "Barty isn't a convincing liar, either. He stammers when he's telling a tall tale. Which leaves me to wonder who paid Miss Barlow a visit Monday night."

She blew over the surface of her tea. "Did you take anything from her office? Something I could hold?"

He'd considered it, especially the trinkets lining her

windowsill. However, Miss Carey had been with him. He'd also recalled how, last autumn, Audrey had accused him of only calling on her for her ability. She'd asked a pointed question, one he still heard in the recesses of his mind: If she did not possess such a useful gift, would he bother with her at all? The truth was, while her gift was extraordinary, so was she. He'd hoped they had made amends, and yet he hadn't wanted to bring her anything now with the expectation that she would help him.

He explained the impossibility of filching anything from the office with the assistant headmistress watching, and then set his teacup down.

"But there is another way you can help," he said, and then launched into one of the reasons he'd come to Violet House. "My father was a good and decent man, so it stands to reason that he would have supported my birth mother just as generously as he did Catherine Marsden."

Audrey lowered her teacup as well, her brow furrowing as she met his expectant gaze. "You believe he financed her finishing school."

"I do."

"Of course. And there might be record of it with his solicitor. Along with more information on April Barlow."

This was why he would come to her, even without her ability. Her quick and clever mind never failed to astonish.

"As you are acquainted with my father's former solicitor, I hoped you might conjure a way to speak to him. Gain access to his files," Hugh explained.

A grin tugged her lips. "Do you mean Mr. Potridge?"

Potridge was the duke's solicitor, as Hugh had come to know last spring when he'd arrested Fournier.

"Barty cut him loose when he became viscount, but my father and Potridge got along well."

With a small wriggle of excitement, Audrey sat forward. "I could call on him tomorrow. Though I'm not sure how to get my hands on his files."

"I find a distraction always works wonders," he said with a wink. "I'll make sure Sir follows you there and provides one."

Hugh was certain the duchess could find a valid reason for going to his office to begin with. As he tucked into his plate of cold ham, cheese, and biscuits studded with currants, Audrey got to her feet and paced before the fire, likely devising her plan. His eyes lifted toward her time and again, her state of dishabille settling into his body with more weight each time he glanced up. The column of her neck was on display, the lace collar of her nightdress not high enough to obscure it. Her feet, so small and dainty, padded over the carpet as she paced, lost in thought.

The picture of the two of them here, like this, could have been that of any man and his wife. The comfort and ease of it tempted him. But it was a distraction he could ill afford. He needed to stay sharp. The creature comforts of this room, of this food, and most formidably, Audrey herself, was muddling his mind.

He finished his food in several more bites and stood. "My compliments to your cook. I won't need to eat for another day, at least."

Audrey stilled and crossed her arms, as if warding off a chill. Looking slightly out of her depth, she gestured toward the boudoir. "You can rest in there tonight. A maid will be in at dawn to build up the fire, but she won't enter the boudoir."

"I can't stay."

Audrey sealed her lips. "You're not leaving?" Before he could reply, she continued, "Where else will you go? It is freezing outside, and it's dangerous, Hugh. They're looking for you."

"They're not going to find me," he said, a little amused by her fretting. She, however, was not amused in the least.

"Your overconfidence is arrogant."

"Your lack of it in me is wounding," he replied.

"There is no need to be heroic. Violet House is safe. You can hide here better than out there." She swung an arm toward the window in which he'd entered. "Better yet, flee. Go to the Continent."

His pride absorbed the hit, though he winced. "I am not hiding, nor will I flee. I need to find Eloisa's killer and clear my name. I can't do that if I'm huddling under blankets in your boudoir."

"You're being irrational," she said, color creeping up her neck. But it wasn't the spirit of anger beginning to grip her. He saw what it truly was in the beseeching glare of her eyes: fear.

Against his own counsel, he crossed the room to stand closer to her. "I know this city. I know how and where to hide. Trust me, Audrey."

She closed her eyes, as if to control her own flaring temper and panic. His hand lifted of its own volition, it seemed, for it was suddenly cupping her cheek. The coarse pad of his thumb met no resistance as it brushed along her skin, warm and velvet soft. Her lashes parted, and twin pools of blue appeared dusky in the changing firelight.

"If they find you, they'll arrest you," she whispered, voice tremulous. "You'll hang."

He gave up the struggle to keep his distance and palmed her other cheek, now far too close. "I won't let that happen."

"I won't either," she said. The panic and fear ebbed from her eyes, replaced with something just as dangerous—stubborn determination. Which for the Duchess of Fournier usually resulted in rash behavior, heedless of any potential peril.

"I am putting you in danger by just being here." His fingertips ran lightly over her hair, down the glossy plait of her braid. "Asking you to visit Potridge and steal files is reckless."

"No. Please, I won't be coddled." Audrey pressed her hands flat against his chest. Surely, she felt the mad charge of his heart-beat under her palms. "If I were the one wanted for murder, you wouldn't shy away from a bit of danger to help me...would you?"

The answer to that was as palpable as his desire for her, which was quickly flooding his good sense. "I'd tear this city down before I let anything happen to you."

The pleased grin bowing her lips had barely formed before Hugh captured her mouth with his. Audrey's hands curled into his waistcoat, pulling him closer rather than pushing him away. After months of shoving aside every errant thought of her—of having one more finger of whisky so that his mind might not drift to her as he lay abed, waiting to fall asleep; of assuring himself repeatedly that there were other women out there in the world who would manage to hold a candle to the duchess—Hugh all but dissolved when she parted her lips and met his tongue with her own. Sweet God in heaven. He'd missed her. Missed her voice, her smell, her presence, her taste.

He met no resistance as he clutched her against him, the soft yet firm impression of her body pulled flush against his. No words were needed to understand her craving; it was mutual. And here they were, in the shelter of her bedchamber, alone, a long night stretching out before them.

The knot in the sash closing her banyan slipped apart effortlessly under his fingers, and with a groan of pleasure, Hugh slid his hands over her hips and closed around the small of her back. The warmth of her skin reached through the thin linen nightdress. He couldn't tear his lips from hers, and Audrey continued to send pangs of desire straight to his groin as she deepened the kiss. Undoubtedly, she felt his arousal, but she didn't retreat. She wasn't afraid.

There was nothing to stop him from lifting the hem of her

nightdress and freeing her of it. Nothing to stop him from laying her upon the four-poster behind them and making love to her as he'd longed to, almost from the first time they'd met. Her fiery tongue, her resolve to see through whatever task she set her mind to, no matter how thorny or dangerous or complicated, and that unnamable, enigmatic pull between them, had finally driven him to his knees.

"Stay," she whispered as her lips parted from his, if only for a second.

He explored the lush curves of her backside and nearly tumbled headfirst into the black abyss of lust. One glaring truth kept him clinging to the edge of the cliff: She was a virgin. Despite having been married for three years, she had never lain with a man. And as soon as the duke cropped up in his addled brain, the tolling of reason swiftly followed.

"I can't," he gritted out. Before her lips could draw him back, he pressed them to her forehead. They each breathed heavily, arms still entwined.

The last time he'd seen her, in November, he'd explained why he could not be her lover. Though they would sate each other's desires, it wouldn't be *enough*. He wanted all of her, not just the part of her that would come unraveled in his arms in a bedroom somewhere. And more importantly, if she were ever to get with child, the baby would legally belong to Fournier. *No*, Hugh would never allow another man to raise his son or daughter.

Nothing had changed.

Except that now he was a fugitive from the law. Which made spending the night with Audrey even more unwise.

She slowly disentangled herself from his arms and with trembling hands, retied the sash of her robe. "Is there someone? A woman who you..."

"No." He wanted to take her into his arms again but held himself in check. "Not for some time now."

If that was any relief to her, he couldn't read it on her suddenly restrained expression. Her cheeks were flushed, her lips swollen.

Hell, he needed to leave. The frozen air outside would do him good.

"Douse your lamp so that anyone watching the house won't see me leave through the window, and lock it after," he instructed, turning to gather his coat and hat.

She said nothing as she turned down the lamp. The room turned to near pitch-black as he put on his coat and hat, and then opened the window. There was no moonlight, no visibility at all as he climbed through and maneuvered himself onto the thick branch of the plane tree. He heard Audrey slide the sash into place and engage the lock, but could not see her. He was grateful for that, at least, as he continued down the tree, to the ground, and then darted away.

ELEVEN

The law offices of Potridge, Chadwick, and Garrison on Gloucester Street in Pimlico were a touch finer than Audrey had anticipated. As she showed herself through the front door of the limestone building and met with a clerk, she ascertained that Mr. Potridge and his associates, though tradesmen, had either been born into means or they made a fine business as solicitors to any number of men, titled or not. It made sense that the upper classes would only entrust their business to those who nearly matched them in status. As the clerk dipped his head in respect and then dashed off to inform Mr. Potridge of her presence, Audrey fought the urge to squirm and flee the premises.

She'd spent a sleepless night wading through any number of plausible pretexts to arrive here, unannounced, and unaccompanied. The challenge of it illuminated the stark fact that there was no *acceptable* reason for a married woman to visit her husband's solicitor without said husband. Surely Mr. Potridge managed property deeds, wills, and contracts of all sorts, but finding a foothold into which she could insert herself was nigh impossible. It had taken the whole of her sleepless night to come up with a credible, if feeble, story.

Hugh had only been a gentleman by leaving, but the rejection had still stung. Yes, leaving was the right thing to do, and he'd already made it plain why he couldn't be her lover. But that had not stopped her from lying in bed, staring at the ceiling, and imagining what might have happened had he *not* been a gentleman. As the night wore on and dawn crept in, her imagination blazed forward into the realms of impossibilities. *If* she could divorce, *if* she could marry Hugh, *if* they could have a family... And then, it struck her: A plausible excuse for a visit to her husband's solicitor.

"This way, Your Grace," the clerk intoned as he reappeared at the bottom of the stairwell. The offices were upstairs, and Audrey, who had left Greer and Carrigan in the carriage on the curb, ascended after the man. She only hoped Sir was already on Gloucester Street, ready to make some sort of distraction for her, as they'd planned that morning when Greer had whispered that the boy was in the kitchen, insisting on speaking to her. Her housekeeper, Mrs. Trelew, did not approve of the boy, but Greer and Mrs. Comstock had softer hearts.

Audrey's pulse increased the closer she became to enacting her plan. Lying to Mr. Potridge didn't appeal to her, and it was very likely that he would at some point let it be known to the duke that she had been to his offices. Unless, of course, the topic of conversation was so baffling and improper that the poor man couldn't bring himself to utter a mention of it.

The clerk showed her into the spacious office, which overlooked the street and had a plethora of shelving and books, and to Audrey's dismay, several tall filing cases, rather than just a few. She only hoped they were well organized and in alphabetical order.

Mr. Potridge, a man of about sixty, with a head of uncommonly thick white hair and a pair of round spectacles that sat low on the bridge of his nose, was already standing and ready to greet her.

"Your Grace, welcome. I was not aware of your intention to call on our offices." When the clerk shut the door after departing, Mr. Potridge added, "Is everything well with the duke?"

"Yes, he is well," she said, but then wondered if he, for whatever reason, might be aware of Philip's mercurial salivation treatments. There would be no reason for Mr. Potridge to know, would there? Or perhaps he had only noted the duke's frequent poor spells.

Mr. Potridge showed her into a chair and then strode behind his desk. "I confess to be flummoxed by your appearance, Your Grace. It is not ordinary for ladies to come in place of their husbands, you see."

Flummoxing him was exactly what Audrey wished to do, and it spurred her on to know that she'd already had some success.

"I understand, and I apologize for the unexpected visit." Her attention drifted toward the burred walnut filing cases next to his desk. Small labels were affixed underneath each drawer's knob. "However," she went on, "I wasn't at all certain I'd have the courage to go through with it, so to send advance notice would have been...premature."

As she'd hoped, the prepared line snagged his curiosity. "The courage? Whatever do you mean, Your Grace?"

No turning back now. Audrey took a bracing breath and met his gaze.

"Mr. Potridge, I have come so you could advise me on the legal ramifications regarding the passing of the duke's title to an adopted son."

The request lingered in the suddenly silent air. The man

blinked, raised the spectacles on his nose, and parted his lips in awe. "A-adoption?"

"I cannot have my own child, you see. It is a source of great shame that I cannot bear an heir naturally," Audrey went on, the topic of which brought a bright splash of crimson to the man's doughy cheeks. "And if we were to take in a child, adopt him, well, I would like to be certain there is nothing barring him from taking on the title, when the time comes, of course."

Mr. Potridge sat down, then stood up again, clearly agitated. He spluttered a few words before finally blurting a whole sentence. "Does His Grace not wish to be part of this discussion? I say, it would be far more appropriate for me to speak to the duke about this."

Sensing the unfortunate man was close to fleeing the room, she whipped out the *pièce de résistance*—her lacy handkerchief —and pressed it to her nose. She shot to her feet and with more theatrical enthusiasm than she thought she possessed, affected tearful distress as she rushed toward the window.

"I can only imagine what you must think of me, Mr. Potridge," she said, attempting to make her voice thick with emotion. "I have been far too brash. If Philip were to hear of this, he would be so cross with me." On the sidewalk across the street, a gangly boy wearing a white apron over his clothes peered up at the window where she stood. Sir tipped the brim of his cap to her, and then dodged a horse and carriage as he crossed the street.

Audrey turned back to the solicitor, who had edged around the desk, toward the door. Victory in sight, she sniffled. "It is just that I know how desperately the duke wishes to be a father. Are you a father, Mr. Potridge?"

The man adjusted his glasses again. "Yes, yes, I am. I have four children, Your Grace."

"So then you must understand!"

Her unmerited exuberance was well rewarded. Ho all but leaped for the door knob. "Please, Your Grace, don't distress yourself any further. Let me call for some tea—"

Before he could complete his excuse for leaving the room, a building commotion sounded from outside his office. A banging about, distant shouts. Then, a great crash.

"What in the world?" Mr. Potridge opened the door and stuck his head out. With the door open, the ruckus became more audible. Defiant squawks from a pre-pubescent boy were unmistakable. Sir's distraction had commenced.

"Wait here, Your Grace, I will see what this nonsense is about." The solicitor stepped out and shut the door behind him.

Not wasting another moment, she rushed to the door and engaged the lock. Being caught rifling through his filing cases wouldn't do. As the hullabaloo continued on the ground level of the law offices, Audrey went to the cases and scanned the drawers. They were indeed organized alphabetically. She pulled open the drawer for L through N and leafed through the folios in the racking system. She tried to keep her hands steady, her attention on the files and not the chances of Mr. Potridge returning before she was through. Blessing the clerk who kept these files tidy, she saw it: Neatham. Holding her breath, she whisked out the thick folio—and found a second behind it. Both were full to bursting with papers. Blast!

She couldn't take the contents of both. There was only room enough in her reticule for a few folded sheets. She wished she'd thought to bring a larger bag but just taking the reticule had caused no end to Greer's suspicious glances; her maid knew she vastly preferred to employ her skirt pockets rather than wear a reticule's strings around her wrist. She'd kept on her gloves to prevent any errant visions, even though paper was usually quite difficult to read. That only made thumbing through the sheets of paper, parchment, and vellum, all of which were scrawled with all manner of legal jargon in the most confounding of penmanship, that much more difficult.

Sweat erupted on the back of her neck and her vision was beginning to blur with panic when her fingers landed on a thin, bound folio of papers, the green cover tied with string. Scrawled in the top right-hand corner of the folio cover was a name: *A. Barlow.*

Heart thudding to a stop, Audrey itched to tear it open. But voices in the corridor alerted her. One of the men approaching sounded like the solicitor. She folded the stiff folio without care, knowing it would be irreparably creased and crumpled, and shoved it into her reticule.

The knob on the office door jiggled once. Twice. "Your Grace?" Mr. Potridge's muffled voice called. "Your Grace, are you in there?"

Audrey carefully shut the cabinet drawer and hustled to the door, attempting to hide her overstuffed reticule under her cloak.

She didn't need to affect breathlessness when she unlocked the door and opened it, finding her solicitor starting at her, confounded.

"Is it safe?" she inquired, peering into the corridor. "I didn't want that madman barging in."

Mr. Potridge reentered the office, pulling on the hem of his waistcoat, the restrained motion revealing his exasperation. Audrey began to feel sorry for the poor man; he'd certainly not expected so much pandemonium when he left his home this morning.

"Not a madman," he replied. "Just a rapscallion street urchin insisting that we stole his cart, which he'd parked out front!"

Ah. That explained the apron Sir had been wearing. Audrey schooled her expression to match her solicitor's annoyance.

"How absurd," she said.

"Indeed! Harmless in the end, I suppose. Though with all that rumpus, I half wondered if our office was being turned over as Tipper and Sons was the other day."

Audrey frowned. "How do you mean?"

Mr. Potridge returned to his desk, and though she'd closed the cabinet drawer, a niggling fear remained that he'd still notice something amiss. But he paid no attention to his filing system.

"The whole place was ransacked. Files and books scattered everywhere. Happened sometime during the night, so no one was injured, thank the good Lord."

"And Tipper and Sons is...?"

"Another solicitor's office. On Fleet Street," he explained, then waved a hand. "But that is neither here nor there. I've instructed Beckett to bring tea. And then, I think perhaps we should arrange for a time to discuss these matters you've spoken of with the duke?"

For a few minutes, she'd forgotten all about her fabricated reason for arriving at the offices. After peering at the solicitor for a few seconds too long, she grasped his words and straightened her back.

"No! No, no, that is quite all right, Mr. Potridge. I can see that I've been much too hasty. Please, do forget I was ever here," she said, clutching the reticule closer under her cloak and practically running toward the door.

"But Your Grace—"

"I'm sorry that I've wasted your time," she said, again pressing the handkerchief to her nose. "Say nothing to the duke, I implore you." And then, before he could call her back, Audrey fled.

TWELVE

Hugh had one chance. If the lady screamed, it was over.

He'd waited for the carriage at a distance, one eye on Lady Reed's landau and another on the pavements, watchful for foot patrols. It was entirely possible the marchioness had alerted Bow Street after receiving the anonymous note that morning. However, after what Audrey said, about the marchioness deliberately lying to Officer Tyne and withholding information about Eloisa's visit to the soiree, Hugh had gambled on the lady heeding the note's ultimatum: *Be at St. George's at Hanover Square today at one o'clock, alone, or Lady E.'s secret will make the evening editions.*

Whatever Eloisa had been withholding from Hugh, he was willing to bet Lady Reed knew and didn't wish it to be revealed.

Hugh stayed behind a parked cart as Lady Reed's landau pulled to a stop and as she entered the church alone. After waiting until her driver was distracted with the pair of grays at the traces, and until he was certain no foot patrols were present, Hugh then entered the sanctuary.

The muffled quiet of the church had the opposite effect that many claimed was a comfort. With his own pulse thudding in his ears, and his breaths sounding unnaturally ragged and quick, he stood for a few moments behind a column at the entrance to the nave. Fewer than a half dozen people sat scattered among the pews; the pastor in his formal robes was currently in whispered conversation with someone near the front. Lady Reed had slipped into a pew near the back.

He didn't have much time. Risk be damned—he needed answers. Audrey had been right to worry; if he was to be apprehended now, Eloisa's murder would be pinned on him, and he would certainly hang. Barty would see to it. The idea of execution didn't frighten Hugh as much as execution for a crime he didn't commit—and one in which he failed to solve—infuriated him.

He slipped into the pew behind the marchioness's and sat directly behind her.

"Here to make a confession, my lady?" he whispered. Her spine stiffened. Her profile came into view as she turned to see him.

The coiled scarf around his neck, all the way to his chin, and the two-day stubble on his cheeks wouldn't be enough to disguise him. Recognition flashed in Lady Reed's eyes.

"*You*," she hissed.

"I'm going to assume you have a modicum of intelligence, Lady Reed, and that you know that I am not Eloisa's killer. If I were guilty, I would currently be on my way to France instead of risking my neck sitting here with you. I want answers. You were the last person my sister spoke to that night—and *don't* bother to say you did not see her. I know you did." He had cut the lady off as she'd attempted to deny it. She sealed her lips and faced forward again.

Voice hushed, she replied, "I see you've spoken to the duchess."

"Which duchess would that be?" Before she could take a breath to retort, he continued, "You lied to Officer Tyne. Why would you want to conceal Eloisa's visit to you that evening?"

His voice reached no further than her ear; their hushed discussion had not yet drawn the attention of the other parishioners. The marchioness kept her eyes forward.

"If you did not harm Eloisa, prove it to Bow Street," she replied. "Leave me out of it."

"I plan to prove it. Odd...I would think you'd like her killer to be apprehended too. Unless you're protecting the person." A thought struck him. "Or are the killer yourself."

She twisted, gray eyes spearing him. "I would never! Eloisa was my friend's child."

The marchioness was careless with her pitched voice and heads turned in their direction. Hugh gritted his molars, lowering his chin to obscure his face with the brim of his hat. "Is that why she came to you?" he asked.

Lady Reed had been friends with the former viscountess? He hadn't known; then again, he'd deftly avoided his father's wife when he'd been younger. "Eloisa asked for your help, and yet you refused her."

"You know nothing, Mr. Marsden."

"I know Eloisa was in London to harm Lord Neatham's reputation and upend his life. I know she had a secret that she wished to be made public," he said, wishing he could view the marchioness's expression while he spoke. "And I know if the murderer suspects Eloisa told you anything of value, your life could be in danger."

Silence followed. She made no quick denial, no comment at all. In the quiet, he sensed a new reserve in her; some notion she had not yet considered.

"Tell me what she wanted from you," he pressed.

The curious glances from the other parishioners had turned

away from them when the marchioness spoke, this time with caution.

"It was terrible timing. I don't know what she was thinking coming to me in the middle of a soiree."

Hugh thought Eloisa's choice of time and place had either been intentional, and a way to agitate Lady Reed and force her hand, or she had been desperate, with no other choices available to her. But now that the woman was talking, he kept his lips sealed.

"I hadn't seen her in years." A note of wistfulness revealed she'd cared about Eloisa. "When my butler informed me that she was there, wishing to speak to me in private, I couldn't comprehend it. At first, I wondered if her aim was to speak to Colonel Trenton."

"Thomas?"

"He was supposed to be at the soiree," she explained. Then, with a flap of her hand, "But he never came. Perhaps now that he's landed himself a bride-to-be, an evening at some stuffy party paled in comparison to an evening at a gentlemen's club."

Or a gaming hell. Hugh preferred to think of Thomas as little as possible, but he suspected his youngest half-sibling frequented the demimonde more robustly than he did his gentry peers.

Audrey had mentioned that he was betrothed, too, but Hugh had no interest in hearing more on the topic. Thomas, five years Hugh's junior, had always been the odd man out. The clinger-on. When they'd been children, he'd glued himself to Eloisa's shadow. Though just a year older, she'd been more of a mother to him than their own mother, the cold and aloof viscountess.

Joanna Neatham had emphatically detested Hugh, and for good reason, he supposed. Her antipathy toward her own children, however, had been a bit more perplexing. At least they'd had a father who'd shown them affection. Of course, sharing their father with Hugh had caused no end to the friction between the four of them.

But Thomas... The viscountess had called him simple. Their father had claimed he was merely reserved and remote, but deep down, Hugh suspected the viscount knew there was something more than just a little odd with his youngest child.

"She didn't want to see Thomas," Hugh surmised. "She wanted something from you."

The marchioness paused to take a shallow breath. "I was a good friend to Joanna. When my own niece, Lila, became the new viscountess, I ought to have been pleased."

Hugh waited, his skin prickling.

"Mind you, I don't know anything for certain," she prefaced, "but as Joanna lay dying, she told me something. A confession."

Hugh recalled those days vividly. The family physician had informed them that the viscountess had tumors of the breast and that they had likely spread to other parts of her body. They were inoperable, so all she could do was make her peace with dying. It had been a drawn-out hellscape, the viscountess wasting away in a remarkable amount of pain until the viscount had demanded the physician give her as much laudanum as possible. She'd passed away soon after that, in all probability of an overdose. It had been a blessing.

"She was delirious, of course, and so I've never been certain if it wasn't all fantasy, but Joanna confessed that...that Bartholomew..." She looked down to her hands. Hugh, now leaning forward in anticipation, saw she had crumpled her handkerchief in her clenched fingers. "That he might not be the rightful heir."

She barely whispered those last few words, and yet they tunneled into Hugh's ears and grew thorns. Each one burrowed, multiplying as they formed a tangled route back to

Eloisa and her unexpected visit earlier that week at Bedford Street.

"How is that possible?" he asked.

The viscount had married Joanna, and just under a year later, Barty had been born. From what Hugh had always been told, just four months after that, Catherine Marsden and her infant son had come to Neatham House. She was to be nanny to baby Bartholomew, and her own newborn was to be raised alongside the Neatham heir. The viscountess's displeasure and humiliation nearly brought the whole house down, but the viscount refused to turn Nanny Catherine or the child out. Instead, he brought the babe on as a ward. Everyone knew the truth from then on. Neither Fitzgerald Neatham nor Catherine Marsden ever denied it, either.

However, now that Hugh knew about April Barlow, he wondered why Catherine had happily taken on the censure for having had an affair with the viscount, especially among the servants at Neatham House; she had never been popular with them. Had his father paid her handsomely? The notion sent his stomach toward his kneecaps, making him nauseous.

"It *isn't* possible," the marchioness said. "The cancer had taken Joanna so thoroughly, you see, and I dismissed her ramblings...but Eloisa, she must have overheard. The girl was around ten years old, I think, and perhaps her mother's anguished cries have always haunted her the way they have me."

Hugh sat back heavily into the pew. "This is what she wanted to speak to you about?"

"She wanted me to come forward with Joanna's confession," she replied crisply. "The absurdity of it! Calling Bartholomew's title into question because of a fevered deathbed confession made nearly two decades in the past? Never!"

Again, her voice had started to rise in step with her agitation. This time, the pastor stood, concluding his conference with the other parishioner. *Damn it.* Hugh could not stay any longer.

"Now you understand why I could not tell Officer Tyne that I'd seen Eloisa," Lady Reed said swiftly. "To have been in her presence so shortly before her death...and if I were to let something slip about the conversation...I am not very adept at lying, Mr. Marsden. I'm much better off if I simply keep my lips sealed."

As soon as the pastor started up the aisle toward their pews, Hugh stood. His time was up. "Someone knew Eloisa was at your home and wished to stop her from calling Barty's legitimacy into question."

"By killing her?" the marchioness gasped, turning to glare at him.

"What do you know about April Barlow?"

The lines in her face deepened as she scowled. "April Barlow? Who in the world is that? What does she have to do with this?"

It wasn't an act of ignorance. Hugh pulled his hat lower. "She is someone I need to find. Be on your guard, Lady Reed. Until the murderer is caught, do not go anywhere alone. You know more than you think you do."

With that, he exited the pew toward the transept aisle, away from the approaching pastor.

THIRTEEN

Audrey burst through the front door to Violet House. She needed to speak to someone she could trust, and of course, Philip came first to mind. He not only knew about Hugh and trusted that he wasn't a killer, he also would not have Audrey arrested for stealing files from Mr. Potridge's office—though, he would be terribly cross with her for it.

She would gamely endure his reproach, however, if he could just help her make sense of the files that she'd pored through on the carriage ride back to Curzon Street.

"Is all well, Your Grace?" Greer had inquired as soon as Audrey had climbed into the carriage. She'd been breathing rapidly, having just practically run from the offices.

"Of course," she'd answered, ripping the folio labeled with Miss Barlow's name from her reticule. "I am just eager to leave Pimlico."

She'd unwound the toggle and string and started shuffling through the papers, holding them to the window for better light. Some of the scrawled penmanship had faded or smudged. Dates from nearly thirty years ago had been inked onto lines next to signatures from Lord Neatham and Miss Barlow and on one, Miss Catherine Marsden.

Audrey read through the files several times on the ride. A contract for the viscount to pay an annual sum of two hundred pounds to Miss April Barlow was dated May of 1793. Another agreement for his estate to pay Catherine Marsden a sum of one hundred pounds per annum for the "care and keeping of male child aged 6 months until said child reaches seventeen years" was dated the same month and year. A letter from Miss Barlow, dated November 1812, was a request that the Neatham estate cease payments to her as she was aware the viscount had recently died. Her wish, she wrote, was that the annuity instead be directed to the viscount's ward, Hugh Fitzgerald Marsden.

Fitzgerald. Audrey felt a twinge of intimacy at learning his middle name. But it was the fact that Fitzgerald was the late viscount's given name that got her ears chiming as Carrigan closed in on Curzon Street. And that Hugh had been six months old at the time Catherine Marsden took him on as her own child.

It was more than apparent now, from these files, that April Barlow was Hugh's birth mother, and that Catherine Marsden was given the child to raise. The viscount financially supported both women, and generously. But...why had it taken *six months* for Miss Barlow to bring baby Hugh to Neatham House?

"Barton," she said to her butler as he approached in the foyer. A footman was relieving her of her cloak, the badly creased folio returned to her reticule, still clutched in her hand. "Is the duke at home?"

Barton bowed. "Yes, Your Grace. He and a guest are in the study."

A guest? Audrey tempered her disappointment as she climbed the stairs. Hopefully the guest, whoever it was, would not stay much longer. Possible ideas and explanations for the folio's papers were swirling around in her brain, and she wanted to dispel and rationalize them. Philip would be perfect for such a task.

He would, of course, demand to know how she'd learned about April Barlow, and when he heard about Hugh's late-night visit, he would certainly be peeved. But she despised keeping secrets from Philip and wanted to be as honest with him as she could be.

She entered the study, its doors slightly ajar. Male voices came from within, reaching her ears before she could see into the room. Audrey drew to a stop as soon as her eyes settled upon the duke and his guest. They stood shoulder to shoulder in front of a painting, a Titian that had been in the Fournier family for well over a century. At first, they did not see Audrey entering the study and continued to gaze up at the Titian. When Philip turned his head to look at the other man—an inch shorter, trim, with dark blonde hair—in the mere seconds before he spied Audrey from the corner of his vision, she recognized something upon his expression. Admiration. Interest. Attraction.

Both men turned, now aware of her presence, and she pushed a smile onto her face.

"Audrey, darling." Philip set his drink on a table as he came to greet her. He took hold of her arms and shuffled her forward with awkward gusto. "I'm glad you're here. I'd like to introduce you to someone. An old friend from my Cambridge days."

The man came forward for his introduction and her stomach dipped—if he was a Cambridge friend, he might occupy Philip's afternoon for longer than Audrey hoped. Philip tended to luxuriate in long conversation with old peers from university, especially when it came to gloriously dull topics like linguistic anthropology and Greek literature, and one that gave her shivers—entomology.

"May I present my wife, Audrey," he said to his friend. "Audrey, may I introduce you to Mr. Frederick Walker."

Her heart rhythm slowed as the man bowed, his hands clasped behind his back. The name chimed through her ears, muffling all sound in the room. Frederick Walker. Freddie. She had heard his name before. It was one she'd committed to memory because of its importance. Because of *his* importance. Freddie Walker had been Philip's first love, and his first lover.

But then, Freddie had been caught in an act of sodomy with another man and arrested. The sentence for such a crime could be as dire as death by hanging, though with Freddie's elevated connections, his sentence had been reduced. Instead, he'd been sent away to an institution rather than a prison. An institution much like Shadewell, where anything deemed unnatural about a person was roundly and categorically stamped out.

And yet, here he was. Standing in Philip's study, no less.

"Mr. Walker, hello. It's a pleasure," she said, finding her voice after some protracted moments. Her delay and the stilted greeting weren't overlooked.

"Your Grace," Mr. Walker replied with a bashful grin. He cast a glance toward Philip, then at Audrey again. "I have been looking forward to meeting you."

"You have?" Her bald surprise caused smothered amusement between the two men. But his comment made it sound as though he and Philip had been in contact. Had they? Audrey suddenly felt overly warm.

"Yes, almost as soon as I returned to London, I heard Philip had married. I wished to meet the lucky lady."

"*Unfortunate* might be a better word," Philip joked.

Oh. Perhaps they had not been in contact then. Still, she was suspicious. Philip had gone behind her back before when there had been no need for him to do so. Last year, if he'd simply come forward and told her that he was seeing St. John, she wouldn't have forbidden him. It was the deception and sneaking about that hurt her feelings and damaged the trust between them.

"And how long have you been in London?" she asked. Her tone was too sharp, revealing her misgivings. Mr. Walker smoothed his cravat and rocked back onto his heels, as if absorbing the punch of her question.

"Perhaps we should sit," Philip said, motioning toward the sofa and chairs.

He met Audrey's eyes with a silent plea to assent. She lowered herself to a sofa cushion, while Philip dutifully took the space beside her. Mr. Walker sat across from them.

"I think we can be frank, Your Grace," Mr. Walker began. "I am aware that you know who I am and where I have been. I want to assure you that I haven't come here to stir any unrest."

"Then why have you come?" She'd softened her voice at least a little. But for this man to be here, with the history and scandal that surely was still attached to him, was a risk. Oddly, Philip, so averse to any risk, any scandal, looked entirely too unperturbed.

"Mr. Walker's circumstances have recently changed," Philip said, but she could sense his hesitancy. He looked to his guest with a clear hope that he would elaborate and save him. Mr. Walker acquiesced.

"These last many years, I've been at Holliston House, an institution in Wales. No better than a prison, but I suppose eight years hard labor transmuted to eight years at a mental institution had a few advantages. Very few, but that is neither here nor there. I won't disturb you with any details of such unsavory places."

She had not heard of Holliston House before, but those sorts of places, much like Shadewell, were little discussed. Even Bethlem Hospital, so close to London proper, just across the river, was not a topic of conversation in polite society. And as Mr. Walker wished to shield her from the realities of the institution, it appeared that Philip had not told him anything about her time at Shadewell. He'd kept his vow to her.

"Eight years?" she said. The numbers didn't make sense. Philip at been at Cambridge a decade ago. Mr. Walker should have been released before now.

"Yes, well, my father decided against my return."

Her stomach cinched. "I see." It wasn't unlike the power her mother and uncle had held over her. They had paid Shadewell to keep her for two years, and Mr. Walker was correct—it wasn't unlike a prison.

"Fortunately, the bastard is now dead," Philip said as he glowered into his drink. Audrey stared at him, agape.

"Philip!"

"I won't apologize."

"And you shouldn't," Mr. Walker agreed. He wore a resigned grimace. "My father was not a kind man. He wasn't a good man. I'm not sorry he's gone. Neither is my brother, who, thankfully, is in possession of a heart. He inherited everything, and that included command over my placement at Holliston House. He brought me home."

Now that she had calmed a little, she saw faint shadows under Mr. Walker's eyes. He did appear a bit too thin, his cheekbones pronounced. He hadn't been free of his prison for very long, she guessed.

"I am glad for you," she said, and genuinely meant it. No one deserved such treatment.

"Thank you," he said, the mood lightening. "After so long in the countryside, London is a feast for the senses. It's a bit overwhelming, if I am honest." He stood up abruptly. "I should take my leave."

Philip got to his feet quickly. "I'll see you out."

"No need," Mr. Walker said. Then, after another moment's hesitation, "I will call on you again soon."

Audrey watched her husband attempt to mask his pleasure. Anyone else might not have seen it, it was so subtle.

"Soon, then," he agreed, and then remained standing as Mr. Walker let himself out of the study.

Audrey raised a brow, still observing Philip. He stared at the door, looking more vulnerable than she'd ever seen him. His lips twitched toward a grin. But then he seemed to recall her and met her gaze.

"I presume you have questions," he said, subduing his smile. He settled down on the cushion Mr. Walker had been seated on, across from her.

"You met with Mr. Walker at Brooks's last night," she said, recalling Philip's mention of an old Cambridge mate at dinner the evening before. She'd been caught up in anticipation for Hugh's midnight visit, so she'd forgotten all about it. Until now.

"Yes."

Philip had returned from his club at dawn. Or perhaps he and Mr. Walker had gone elsewhere.

"Are you going to see him again?" she asked.

He rubbed his hands together—a nervous tic—as he considered her question. "I would like to. If you are amenable?"

"If it would make you happy." She considered leaving it at that, but then decided to vent her reservation rather than hold it in. "But Philip...there could be talk. His past is quite scandalous."

"It is," he sighed, then pinched the bridge of his nose. "Perhaps it isn't wise. I'll need to think on it some more." He stood and broke toward his desk. "Heaven knows I'm being a hypocrite even considering it."

Audrey got to her feet. "How do you mean?"

Philip flung out an arm. "I warned you not to take Marsden

as a lover because of his past, didn't I? Now look what's happened. I was right to have such reservations. Any association with him now would prove ruinous. I should listen to my own counsel."

At Hugh's name, she recalled the reason she'd come to the study in the first place. The folios. Her reticule ribbons were still wrapped around her wrist, the papers inside potentially vital. It was on the tip of her tongue to ask Philip about them, but she swallowed the urge. If she brought out the folios, she'd have to tell Philip about Hugh's visit the night before. He'd be furious. She wasn't in the mood for an argument. She also didn't want to hear Philip forbid her from helping Hugh again. Furthermore, she didn't want to have to tell Philip that she would not be heeding his command.

"I should leave you to your thoughts," she said, hoping she didn't sound too eager to flee. "I'll be in my study."

Wrapped up as he was in his own state of affairs, Philip didn't try to convince her to stay. Audrey kissed his cheek and then hurried toward the back of the house, where her small study was located. It was her favorite room in Violet House. Though half the size of Philip's study, it was feminine and brighter, with tall windows overlooking the small kitchen garden. It was cozy rather than austere, and it always gave her the impression of being far away from the rest of the world. Far away from London and the ton and even her own persona as Duchess of Fournier. Here, she could just be Audrey.

She entered the study and let out a great exhale as she shut the door behind her. The room wasn't as sunny as usual, the curtains not having been drawn. They billowed a little, as if in a breeze. The odd chill of the air registered too late.

Arms grabbed at her from behind. A man's coarse hand clamped down over her mouth while his brawny arm pinned both her arms into place at her sides. His ungloved palm muffled her scream, and though she squirmed to get free, he was too big and strong for her fight to make any difference. Unlike the night before, when Hugh had come up behind her, this man was rough. Unyielding.

"Don't struggle, lamb," the unfamiliar voice said softly into her ear. "You don't want no one to come running to see what's the matter."

She went still. If a footman or maid heard her, they would indeed come to investigate. Philip might as well. This man might have a weapon.

"Good girl." His praise made her stomach roll. The stench of unwashed clothes and the sour tang of urine did as well. "Now, hand them over. The papers. I know you got them."

Her blood slowed, and her ears began to throb. The folios. He'd followed her from Pimlico? Audrey tried to speak, but his hand was still cupping her mouth. The touch of his skin against hers and his pungent odor made her want to gag.

"No screaming," he warned. Audrey nodded, and he slowly lowered his hand. She dragged in a breath.

"Where is April Barlow?" she asked. The folio's contracts all had to do with her. This could be the man who'd paid Miss Barlow a late-night visit and warned her off.

He wrapped both arms around Audrey now, squeezing her back tighter against his front. His lips touched her earlobe. "You're in no position to be asking questions. The files. Now."

Her ribs ached as his grip constricted her ribs even tighter.

"My reticule," she gasped, and she felt his hand scrabbling to free the ribbons from her wrist. She was at least grateful she'd read them on the way back home and not waited until she reached her study.

"Who do you work for?" she asked, even though she sensed he was too astute to give her an answer. Even if he did smell like a horse stall.

The man laughed in her ear. "If you're smart, you'll keep out of this business."

Audrey fought the urge to stomp his foot. How dare he break into her home and manhandle her like this? If she wasn't so worried that Philip or the servants would come running in and scuffle with this miscreant, she'd scratch at his eyes and fight to keep those files.

Before she could do anything, he lobbed her toward the floor. She crashed in an ungainly heap, knocking her knee painfully against the leg of a chair and glancing her temple off the floor. By the time she scrambled back up to her feet, shocked and dizzy, the room was empty. The intruder was gone.

Audrey ran to the billowing curtains and threw them aside to find the open window in which he'd made his escape. On the lawn below, a man in a drab, workaday coat and hat hurdled over a row of snow-capped hedges and disappeared without a backward glance. She didn't so much as glimpse his face.

Audrey swore and slammed the window shut.

FOURTEEN

The door to the row house opened and Hugh fell backward, his resting place suddenly ripped away from him. Sprawled across the rear entrance's threshold, he stared up into the scowling face of his closest friend.

"What in God's name are you still doing in London, you bloody fool?" Thornton hissed as the toe of his boot kicked Hugh's shoulder.

He got to his feet, brushed off the seat of his trousers, and turned to face Grant Thornton. It seemed the good doctor had finally deigned it time to come to his Whitechapel clinic.

"Where the hell have you been?" Hugh asked, his throat dry, his stomach grumbling. He'd spent the night in the back room of a used bookshop on the Strand, compliments of one of Sir's associates who owed him a favor. The associate had a key to his uncle's shop, and assured Sir that no one would be in before eight o'clock in the morning. So, when the shop bell woke Hugh at half six, he'd nearly brought down a whole stack of musty tomes as he rushed to leave through the alley door.

He'd told Sir to meet him at the Whitechapel clinic at nine sharp with whatever information Audrey had managed to find at Mr. Potridge's office. Sir would have gone to Violet House the afternoon before, but he'd unfortunately stopped by Bedford Street to inform Hugh's valet, Basil—who was holding down the residence in Hugh's absence and likely dusting and washing everything to within an inch to its life—that Hugh was still alive. A foot constable placed on watch outside number 19 Bedford Street had seen Sir, and he'd had to run like the devil to lose him. On the off chance he was spotted again, Hugh told him to keep a far step from Audrey until well past nightfall.

"Get inside," Thornton said, pulling him into the kitchen. The spare collection of rooms was run down and sparsely furnished, but the entry level floor of the row house saw plenty of commotion once a week when Thornton opened the doors to the public. He treated all manner of ailing, consumptive, and disease-ridden men, women, and children here, and because he was irrefutably in line for sainthood, he kept coming back for more.

A fire in the cookstove was in the process of heating four large pans of water, and Thornton's nurse, a young woman named Miss Matthews, was busy preparing his instruments. She ignored Hugh after a quick nod hello; he had nothing to fear from her. She'd been with Thornton for a few years, and if she weren't trustworthy, she wouldn't be here at his secret clinic.

Here, Thornton was known only as Doctor Brown. No one in the ton knew of the place, certainly not his father, the Marquess of Lindstrom. That his son was a physician was embarrassing enough; that he would cater to the lower denizens would have caused the gentleman to perish on the spot. At the moment, that made the clinic the perfect place for Hugh to be.

Thornton grabbed the kettle and a tin of black tea. He offered it, and bread and jam or butter, or some bit of food, to all his patients when they came to see him. Many of them were ill from diseases stemming from malnourishment. The food only sated them for a short while, but at least it was something they could depend upon.

"You're in a world of shit, my friend," Thornton said.

"I am aware."

"You need to get out of the bloody country. They *will* hang you." He banged around the kitchen getting Hugh tea, his nurturing soul on full display now. It was rather touching to see his friend in such a state, but it also highlighted the seriousness of Hugh's situation.

Thornton was no coddling sod. He was the sort of friend who told Hugh to toughen up or get the fuck out. Last fall, when Hugh showed up at Thornton's door, his arm in dire need of aid after being impaled with a long blade, his friend had joked about possible sepsis, the risk of permanent injury to the muscles and tendons, and how he might never be able to use his hand again for personal pleasure, all while stitching him up. Now, however, Thornton wasn't joking. He wasn't treating this lightly or with his usual blasé attitude.

"I know a man who can get you to Dover. You can take a packet to Calais," Thornton said as Hugh sawed off a thick slice of bread from a loaf on the table. He took a bite, and with a full mouth, asked, "You think I'm going to run? Give up my life here for something I didn't do?"

"You won't have a life if they find you." Thornton slammed the porcelain teapot onto the table. The dainty pattern of roses didn't fit with this shabby kitchen.

"I am not leaving the country," Hugh said evenly. He swallowed the bread, which instantly quelled the growling of his stomach. "Eloisa was murdered, and I think Barty had something to do with it."

Thornton turned to his nurse, and with his unspoken request, she nodded and left the kitchen. He pulled out the chair across from Hugh at the small table.

"Explain," Thornton said as he sat.

"A few days before she was killed, Eloisa came to me." Hugh then divulged his sister's suggestion that April Barlow was his mother, and about his visits to Sir Roberts's home and the Field Street finishing school.

"I think Barty sent a man to warn off Miss Barlow," he said. "If Eloisa knew of her, surely, he did as well."

"And Miss Barlow is now missing?"

Hugh raised his hands in a gesture of ambiguity. "Perhaps. Or perhaps she is simply hiding somewhere for a little while."

"At Chatham Park?" Thornton suggested, but Hugh had already dismissed that idea. She and her father were not close.

"She has a sister. Sir Robert did not say her name or anything about her." And Miss Carey, the assistant head-mistress, had not known. Hugh imagined April Barlow had revealed very little about her life to the young woman. The lie that Hugh had died as a child continued to spear him. The excuse afforded her a reason to keep the oil portrait on display; but why keep it at all?

"You believe Neatham knew of Eloisa's intent to ruin him," Thornton said, sitting forward, elbows on the table. "And this unknown man who met with Miss Barlow...you think he's the one who killed your sister."

It made the most sense so far. Still, as priggish and mean as Barty had always been, Hugh couldn't quite believe that he would order the death of a sibling. Wishing she had died along-side her infant, as he'd so callously said back at Neatham House, was altogether different than actively ordering her death. Not to mention that Eloisa had been hiding her presence in London from him. He had seemed genuine in his surprise to learn she was in town.

Thornton sat back in his chair. "April Barlow or Catherine Marsden—what does it matter to Barty who your mother is?

How could the discovery of Miss Barlow possibly threaten him?"

Hugh gulped his tea, and as it warmed his belly, he told Thornton of his clandestine conversation with Lady Reed the previous day at St. George's and what the marchioness had imparted about the late viscountess's fear that Bartholomew wasn't the true Neatham heir.

"But there is no basis for it. A little thing called primogeniture ensures no bastard child can ever claim a title," Hugh went on with a wave of his hand. "Besides, I was born months after Barty when my father was already married to Joanna."

Thornton sat still, his coloring suddenly going pale. His lips parted as he continued to stare blankly at Hugh. "You saw Lady Reed? Yesterday?"

"Were you not listening?"

"When was your meeting?"

Hugh tore off another piece of bread, forgoing the knife this time. "Two o'clock. What does it matter?"

Thornton shoved back his chair, the scrape against the bare board floors grating. "Fuck." He raked his fingers through his hair, his distress clear.

Hugh tossed the bread back onto the table. "What is it?"

Before his friend could begin to explain, Hugh knew. The premonition had haunted the back of his mind since leaving the church.

"Lady Reed was found dead last evening," Thornton said, and Hugh's stomach dropped. "Lord Reed said her maid discovered her. She'd been resting in her bedchamber but wouldn't wake. They are saying it was apoplexy or heart failure."

Hugh stared into his drained teacup as frustration simmered. He'd told her to be cautious, to not go anywhere alone. She hadn't thought her own home would be unsafe.

"Or it was a pillow over her face while she slept," Hugh said, closing his hand into a fist.

"Death by suffocation causes burst blood vessels in the eyes, and the state of the victim's tongue can also indicate asphyxiation." Thornton's matter-of-fact way of speaking about anything medical at least felt normal. "If any coroner is intelligent enough to note those findings, her death will be investigated. And bloody hell, Hugh—you were with her. You, a man who is already wanted for another murder that occurred in her home just a few nights before."

"You don't need to remind me."

"Who saw you together?"

He closed his eyes, feeling a sharp pang in his temple at this new blow.

"A pastor, but I doubt he recognized me." Someone clearly had seen them together though. "The killer must have been watching. He was either following me or Lady Reed."

"You would know if you were being followed," Thornton assured him. And he was right. Hugh had been abundantly careful. He also had Sir, whose sharp-eyed observation rivaled the finest officers at Bow Street. Still, he worried.

"I need a favor," Hugh said, with an ill curl of unease.

"If it's within the law." Thornton shrugged. "Or a reasonable inch beyond it."

"Find someone you trust to keep watch over the duchess and Violet House. Night and day."

His friend peered at him, and the scowl he'd met Hugh with on the doorstep made a return. "Why would I need to do that?"

Hugh raked a hand through his hair. "I went to her."

She had doused the lamps to help obscure him as he climbed through her bedroom window, and Sir had scattered the foot patrols, but he might still have been seen.

Thornton swore under his breath and avoided Hugh by

going to the cookstove. The water in the pans was steaming now. "You are an idiot," he muttered.

Hugh didn't think his friend was wide of the mark. "She was at Lady Reed's. She found Eloisa. I wanted to know what she saw."

Among other reasons for wanting to see her.

"I know she was there." Thornton grabbed the simple tweed coat he wore while being *Doctor Brown* from a brass hook and tugged his arms through the sleeves. "She sent word to me about the smoke."

Hugh went still. "She said nothing about that."

A building murmur of voices at the front of the rowhouse indicated his first patients were arriving. Thornton went to the back door, which he no doubt planned to boot Hugh through, into the alley.

Thornton arched a brow. "I am sure the two of you were preoccupied with other...topics."

"Don't be an arse. Nothing has happened, and it won't."

Thornton made a sound in his throat that needed no translation: he didn't believe it. He opened the door, but the prospect of going back out into the frigid cold threatened to glue Hugh's boots to the floor.

"What about the smoke?" Hugh asked, though not just to stall. The newssheets had mentioned the thick brume as well. It sounded like a tactic the killer used to clear the room and give him an advantage in sneaking up on Eloisa.

"The duchess and I attend lectures at the Lyceum, and several weeks ago Alexander and Jane Marcet, both chemists, were presenting a talk on Mrs. Marcet's book, *Conversations on Chemistry*."

Hugh refrained from rolling his eyes. "Riveting, I'm sure."

A few months ago, when Thornton mentioned seeing Audrey at the Lyceum, Hugh had been slightly envious, but not surprised. Staid, common society outings would not interest the duchess. Her sharp mind would be drawn to information, even if to Hugh the topic was absurdly dull.

"I think I drooled a bit when I nodded off, if I'm honest," Thornton admitted. "But there were a few demonstrations, and one was the combination of several elements inside a tube that produced a small smoke bomb. The odor was quite strong and the haze so thick, the hall was cleared for a short while."

"This was several weeks ago?" Hugh asked, intrigued.

"About a month," he replied with a nod. "The duchess had planned to attend but was unable."

"What did she ask of you?"

"Just my thoughts on the matter, to see if there could be a connection. I sent a request to the Marcets to speak to them more about this device they set off. I have an appointment with them this afternoon." He winked. "If I nod off while listening to them in their home, I shall lay the blame on you."

"Why not? I'm already accused of worse." Hugh shook his head and grinned.

Thornton dug into his waistcoat pocket and held up a key. "There is a room upstairs, if you find yourself in need."

Hugh thanked him and took the key. Outside, he flipped the collar of his great coat against a raking wind.

"I will put a man on Violet House," Thornton called after him. "I'll also find out what I can about Sir Robert's other daughter and her whereabouts. Just stay out of sight for now."

The door shut, and Hugh continued down the alley. He hadn't taken a few strides before Sir fell into step with him, appearing as if belched up from the center gutter.

"Got some bad news, Mister Hugh."

"Lady Reed is dead. I've heard." Ahead in the alley, a coal cart driver was backing up his load, blocking the way. Hugh slowed and took a glance over his shoulder. "Sir, are you certain no one has been following me?"

"Sure, I'm sure." Sir's voice pitched high as if offended. "But the bad news ain't about some dead lady. The duchess nicked some papers."

Hugh looked down the boy, whose hands were empty. "Where are they then?"

"Gone."

"What do you mean? How?"

"She don't know who it was, but a man was waiting for her in her house. The blighter took them papers and scarpered."

Alarm streaked through his veins. Regret chased it. "Did the bastard hurt her?"

Sir shook his head. "Nah, she's just steamed. So am I. Nearly got m'self knocked about at that solicitor's place, helping her get 'em. They thought I was the footpad what turned over another solicitor's place the night before. They was on their guard, they was."

Acid filled Hugh's throat when he thought of some faceless intruder waiting for Audrey inside Violet House. It could have been the same person who went after Lady Reed, if indeed she hadn't died of natural causes, which Hugh thought likely.

This was his doing. He'd asked her to steal his father's files, and evidently, someone had been watching.

Hugh frowned. "What other solicitor was turned over?"

Sir shrugged. Perhaps it wasn't important, but two solicitors' offices being rifled through in so many days seemed an odd coincidence.

"The duchess said she read the papers 'fore they were taken and that it's real important she see you," Sir continued. "She's got a ball tonight and wants you to go."

The vitriol Hugh had been spewing at himself abruptly cut off.

"I cannot go to a ball," he said as the coal cart straightened out and an opening in the alley appeared. What was Audrey thinking? She knew he couldn't show his face in public, let alone at a ball.

Sir overtook him and turned around, bringing Hugh up short. He stopped just before slamming into the boy.

"Corner of Hart and Duke streets, near Grosvenor Square. Show up around nine. Her driver'll find you. The meaty one," Sir ordered. "The duchess insists."

Hugh gritted his teeth. "Of course, she does."

FIFTEEN

"I should have canceled," Genie whispered as she took Audrey's arm and pulled her toward a potted lemon tree. Glossy green leaves and b right yellow fruits hung from the branches, which, in contrast to the frigid, bleak weather outdoors, put Audrey in mind of a tropical island. That had been Genie's intent, and she'd purchased the shrubs from a hothouse just for this ball, the first she and Michael had hosted since Charlie's birth last November. Limes and lemons and oranges brightened the ballroom in Lord and Lady Herrick's Grosvenor Square home, and to play upon the theme, the women had been invited to wear gowns in all shades of bright colors. But there was nothing cheery about the crowd that had turned out.

Lady Reed's death was being attributed to the stress and shock of the murder of Eloisa Neatham, but the whispers of the ton suggested that doubts remained. Audrey held reservations about it too, but she'd bit her tongue. In fact, she hadn't done a whole lot of speaking all day. The previous afternoon, instead of rushing from her study to find Philip after the horrid intruder had fled, she'd poured herself a brandy and downed it to stop the quivering of her limbs. The spirits had worked. However, they had also seemed to fuel a simmering fury within her.

She'd been bested. The intruder had followed her to and from Gloucester Street, known what she was taking from Mr. Potridge's office, and with a show of force, had ripped away something that might have helped Hugh's case. It left her stunned and furious for the rest of the day. But she hadn't been able to bring herself to confess to Philip about any of it. Each time she considered trying, she would think of Freddie Walker's visit, and her tongue would suddenly turn to lead. The wrath she felt over the intruder and the loss of the folio would temper under a kinking sensation in her belly.

Philip's first love had returned. If he took back up with Freddie, began a clandestine affair, she would undoubtedly see him less. Time with the man he loved would hold more significance than time spent with her, his best friend. Would she become a duty to him? Would their time together be something he simply needed to endure, while he warmed with anticipation of his moments with Freddie?

The twisting of her stomach wasn't jealousy in the traditional sense; it was something else, and it was utterly confusing. So, she avoided it. Avoided Philip and the whole topic. He'd gone out the previous night, presumably with Mr. Walker, and Audrey had entertained another nighttime caller knocking upon her bedchamber window. This one, however, was much scrawnier.

"Got them papers, duchess?" Sir had asked as he perched in the open window frame.

Hugh's associate turned out to be satisfying company for her surly complaints, and the boy even taught her a few new insults—though she wasn't entirely sure what a "fat-skulled bag of cobbler's awls" was. Though, she imagined it wasn't anything complimentary. Audrey had been prepared for Sir's visit at least, and before the boy left, explained her plan for a furtive meeting with Hugh.

"He's gonna think you're a goosecap."

She'd blinked, confused. "It has nothing to do with birds, Sir." The boy had only laughed and tipped his hat before scrambling back to the ground.

Now, she stood in Genie's ballroom, an eye on the grandfather clock as her sister-in-law fretted over the timing of her party.

"This is exactly what everyone wanted, Genie," Audrey said over the elegant strains of the violins and flutes. "A gathering in which to gossip about other people's misfortunes."

Invitations had gone out long before Saturday's disaster of a soiree at Lady Reed's, and the marchioness's death could not have been predicted.

The notes of an oboe filtered through the music, giving it a solemnity that it could have done without.

"I suppose you're right," Genie conceded, then looked askance at Audrey. "My, but you are awfully cynical."

She sipped her punch. "If by cynical you mean realistic."

The sea of vivid greens, yellows, oranges, and pinks parted, revealing a glimpse of Cassie across the ballroom's parquet. She wore a shimmering ginger gold gown, which highlighted the streaks of auburn in her dark hair.

"She looks beautiful," Audrey said, noting the pink flush of her cheeks. "And happy."

She tried to ignore a pinch of jealousy. It had taken leaving Violet House to induce a smile upon Cassie's lips. But then, perhaps the reason for that smile was simply her present company. She stood within a small circle of men and women, though Cassie's attention kept drifting toward a handsome, fair-haired young man. He seemed to be speaking to her for the most part as well. His golden curls and the wry bow of his lips as he grinned at Philip's sister reminded Audrey of someone else.

"Genie, isn't that young William?"

"Not so young any longer. My baby brother has at last come out of university and is living life as a gentleman about town."

Genie gazed upon her youngest sibling with marked affection. Just shy of thirty, Genie was the eldest of five. After her mother died a decade before, she had assumed the role of mother to her four brothers. It was one of the reasons she'd taken so long to settle down herself; she'd been far too preoccupied with their rambunctious antics.

The family had been left on the brink of impoverishment after their father's death when they learned of his many unwise investments and business ventures, so Genie's union with Michael had been a boon. Her other brothers, now all in their twenties, worked in various business, but Michael had taken charge of William's education.

"He looks smitten with Cassie, doesn't he?" Genie said, her concern over the gloomy state of the gathered crowd lifting.

Audrey saw the interest lighting his eyes as well. She peered at Genie. "He isn't aware, is he?"

Genie cut her an alarmed glare. "No! Of course not. I love my brothers, but I am loyal to Michael and his wishes. Cassie's secret is safe with me."

Heat rushed to Audrey's cheeks. "I didn't mean to suggest otherwise," she said quickly, feeling instantly foolish for having asked. "I'm sorry, I'm not myself these last few days."

"How could anyone expect you to be, with what you've gone through?" Genie laid a gentle hand, sheathed in a pomegranate red silk glove, upon her forearm. "My dear, you found yet another dead body. And how wretched you must feel knowing Officer Marsden is behind it."

Audrey moved out from under her sister-in-law's well-intentioned hand. "He isn't."

Genie's gaze narrowed at her vehemence. "You are certain?"

"I am. Quite." Audrey couldn't expect anyone who did not know Hugh to have that same level of reassurance.

Her driver Carrigan, however, had been one person she'd predicted would. And correctly. With his help, she'd arranged another meeting with Hugh for after the ball. She might not have the papers she'd taken from Mr. Potridge's office, but she had them committed to memory. Come ten o'clock, she anticipated finally being able to discuss them. Anticipation made her skin itch and her feet restless, though she had no desire to dance. Not that anyone would ask her anyhow.

"I wish the duke could have joined you this evening," Genie said, as though she'd been privy to Audrey's thoughts.

"He had a previous engagement."

Genie upheld the vague excuse with an indulgent laugh. "Some meeting over brandy and cigars at a club, no doubt."

Philip's unexpected absence meant that she would now see Hugh alone; she'd planned to tell Philip about the arranged meeting just before ten, and to do so right here, in the ballroom, which would require him to tame his fury. And when the three of them were finally together, Hugh's presence might have further tempered the duke's ire when she confessed about her outing to Pimlico and then the intruder.

Across the room, Cassie and William parted company, he bowing and Cassie making a polite curtsey. As she came toward her sisters-in-law, her cheeks were flushed pink, her eyes glittering.

"William has asked for my next two dances," she squeaked when she reached them.

"Oh, how lovely!" Genie said, likely already envisioning a summer wedding at Greenbriar, their country estate in Kent.

"He is quite dashing," Audrey said, thankful to have something to encourage Cassie about for the first time in months. Even if he'd resembled a toad, she would have said it, if only to keep her grinning so brightly.

"He is," she agreed, sneaking a look back at him. But then her grin ebbed. "But perhaps... I don't know. He is very sweet."

Genie and Audrey exchanged a quick glance before Cassie faced them again, her girlish grin now gone completely. "What if he finds out?"

Audrey took her hand and squeezed. "Do not allow fear a foothold," she said. "He is clearly taken with you. Enjoy your dances. That is all you need to think about right now."

Genie was quick to agree, which seemed to bolster Cassie's confidence. At least for now. But the secret she carried, along with so much grief and regret, was something that might continue to haunt her. Perhaps for a long time.

She moved off to speak with a few other young ladies, and Audrey again eyed the grandfather clock. The hour was nearly upon her. Genie pouted when she announced she was taking her leave for the evening, but it was all in good humor. And besides, as hostess, she had a duty to mingle. Audrey had monopolized enough of her time.

As Greer fetched her pelisse and the carriage was called, Audrey's nerves seemed to grow barbs. As did her guilt.

"I know it is incredibly rude of me, Greer, and it's wickedly cold tonight, but would you join Carrigan in the box for the ride to Violet House?"

Her maid blinked, only pausing at the odd request a moment before nodding. "Of course, Your Grace."

If she suspected something afoot, she made no remark about it. Carrigan, too, acted as he always did, handing her up inside and latching the door shut. The only difference tonight was the inside of the carriage. The single small interior lantern was unlit, and for good reason.

"Sir said you were unharmed. Is that true?"

Hugh's voice came through the darkness to her immediate left. She had taken the forward-facing bench out of habit, and apparently, Hugh had selected the same one. Audrey turned toward him, but could see nothing, her eyes not yet having adjusted. Carrigan had also pulled the window hangings, so streetlamp lights could not enter.

She was taking no risks. After dropping her off about an hour ago, her driver had traveled a few streets over to collect Hugh and hide him within the carriage before traveling back to the mews behind Michael and Genie's home to wait with the other conveyances and drivers. The foot brazier had been stoked, and the orange glow of the coals through the grate was the only bit of light in the carriage.

"He didn't harm me," she said, having anticipated Hugh's discontent.

"When I find who it was, he won't be able to say the same."

The threat was not hollow; Hugh would see it through.

"I would appreciate it if you would at least leave him somewhat conscious so he can feel my palm across his cheek."

"Gladly," he replied. "Is there anything about him you remember? Did you see his face?"

"I didn't. I should have grasped some of his coat to try and see something, some vision. But I'm afraid I was much too startled and frightened." Her mind seemed to need to be clear and calm to be effective with her ability. "He smelled like a poorly mucked horse barn, and he had coarse hands. That's all I can recall."

A beat of silence. Then, Hugh nearly growled, "He put his hands on you?"

The fine hair on her arms lifted. "Only to muffle my scream. Truly, I am unharmed."

He exhaled a rasping sound of fury from low in his throat.

"We don't have long," he said. "Tell me what you found in Potridge's office."

"I will. But first, when is your birthday?" she asked.

"Why, are you throwing me a party?"

"I'm serious, Hugh."

"So am I. I enjoy cake."

"*Hugh*." Audrey sealed her lips when she heard him chuckle. Even though it was dark, she could picture his crooked grin.

"April fifteenth," he answered, humor still lightening his tone.

Audrey, however, felt a stone lodge in her stomach. "Of 1793?"

"That's correct."

Carrigan had started toward Curzon Street, the wheels rattling over the cobbled streets. She had requested him to take a meandering route, to give her more time.

"That can't be right," she whispered as she thought of the contracts she'd read several times the previous day—when she'd still possessed them.

"I assure you, I know my own birth date," Hugh returned.

"But...you see there were two contracts, both drawn and signed in May of that year. One between the viscount and April Barlow, agreeing upon an annual sum. A generous amount. She could certainly have operated her school with it. And the second contract was between the viscount and Catherine Marsden." She paused, recognizing how awkward and painful the details of the contract might be to him.

"Don't stop on account of whatever sentiments you think I am suffering from," he said, deducing the reason for her hesitation.

He was right. There could be no avoiding it. "She was given an annual sum as well for the care and keeping of a male child aged six months until the child reached age seventeen."

Not only had Catherine Marsden not been his birth mother, as he had always believed, she had also been paid to care for him. However, that insult was not what he appeared to focus on.

"Aged *six months*?" he repeated.

She had felt his warmth, his presence, even if in the dark, but now her eyes were beginning to adjust. They made out his brawny figure next to her on the bench.

"I do not believe you were born in April," she whispered. "You would have been one month, not six, if that were the case. Hugh...when was Bartholomew born?"

If her calculations were correct, the answer would be January. He confirmed it. Audrey's heart pounded as the truth came clear. "You were born first."

He shifted, and his clothing rustled.

"Even if that is true," he began, "my father married the viscountess the previous year. I am still a bastard, whether I am older than Barty or not."

More calculations streamed through her mind, and considering how astute the Bow Street officer was, she knew he, too, was working them out.

"If you were born in November," she began, "you were conceived in March or thereabouts, of 1792. When were the viscount and viscountess married?"

He didn't answer straightaway, though Audrey knew he knew.

"May," he finally said, his words soft. "But none of that matters if he and April Barlow simply had a tryst a few months before the wedding."

She took a shallow breath. "What if it was more than that?"

"More?" Hugh turned toward her. "What do you insinuate?" The deep tenor of his voice vibrated down into her bones. If he directed that tone toward anyone else, they might have stiffened and braced for some kind of violence. Audrey, however, only longed to touch him in some way, to soothe him. Hugh knew what she insinuated, but he was becoming angry and didn't want to face the possibility.

Carrigan directed the horses, making a familiar sharp turn. His circuitous route had been far briefer than she'd hoped. They were closing in on Curzon Street.

"You said Sir Robert admitted that they ran off together for a short while," she reminded Hugh. "Do you not think they might have run off to Gretna Green?"

"No." His tone brooked no argument. Audrey ignored it.

"If they married—"

"They didn't."

"But if they had, and then your father left her for whatever reason—"

"He would never have done something so despicable," he interjected.

She forged onward. "His marriage to the viscountess would have been bigamous. Their children, illegitimate. Bartholomew would be ruined. Exactly as Eloisa promised."

There. She'd said it. Audrey drew a long breath and waited for Hugh to respond. She was still waiting when Carrigan slowed to turn into Violet House's half-moon drive.

"You're staying in the stables tonight," she rushed to say. "Carrigan has made a space for you, away from the others."

"I can't. It's too dangerous. There might be someone following me. Lady Reed is dead, and only hours after we met at St. George's. In fact, I've had Thornton place someone on watch outside Violet House, in case my meeting with you has put you in danger too."

His voice was flat, emotionless. He was attempting to avoid what she had said.

"I'm not in any danger, not with foot patrolmen ambling

past Violet House several times an hour. Hugh, please—"

"Was there a certificate of proof in the folio?"

Her cresting hope faltered. "No."

But if they had gone to Gretna Green in Scotland to elope, as eager and desperate lovers often did, there would be record of it in the marriage register there.

"I cannot be heir, Audrey," Hugh said softly. "I do not want the title. I have no desire to challenge Barty for it."

She held her breath as she turned toward him. Her knees brushed against his leg. "I know."

Hugh had been spurned all his life, treated wretchedly by those who thought themselves above him. He'd been exiled from even his lowly place as bastard ward. He despised the ton. The idea of becoming a member of it must have been appalling to him.

"You must find April Barlow," she said. "She is the only one who will know the truth."

If she is still alive. Which begged the question: Why hadn't she been killed that night at the school, rather than just warned off?

"She has a sister," Hugh said. "Thornton is looking into where I can find her."

Audrey nodded. She wasn't close with her own older sister, Millie, but if she were ever in any sort of danger or need, Audrey would never deny her. Despite their past and their many differences, she hoped Millie would do the same for her.

Carrigan drew the horses to a stop. In another moment, he would descend from the driving box and open the door.

"I would sleep better if you stayed," she said. "Please. Carrigan will keep you hidden."

More of Hugh's handsome face was visible now in the dark. He shifted his shoulders so that he faced her on the bench. "Promise me you won't come out to the stables tonight."

She sat straighter, surprised at the request. Even more surprising was that she hadn't realized the temptation lingered in the back of her mind. Hugh had known it before even she.

"Even mule-headed men like me have Achilles' heels," he added. He could see her better too, for he lifted his hand and cupped her cheek.

"You consider me your weakness?" she asked, uncertain how she felt about that. It didn't feel much like a compliment.

"Not at all. It is my desire for you that is my weakness."

Audrey bit her lip, her blood heating at his confession. "I won't come to the stables, if that is what you want."

He exhaled, though it was touched by a soft groan. His thumb caressed her cheek, and through the dark, his lips found hers. She leaned forward, the press of his mouth like a magnet. The stirring need for another ravenous embrace, similar to the other night, whisked away all thought, all reason.

But Hugh maintained reason for them both. Before the kiss could intensify any further, he pulled away and rested his forehead against hers.

"What I want is for you to be safe from danger. From now on, keep a weapon on your person at all times. A knife, if not a muff pistol. Understood?"

She nodded, her pulse quickening. She was a terrible shot, and she wasn't sure she could wield a knife well either.

"Audrey, when this is all over—" he started to say, but they had taken too long. The door opened, and Carrigan announced he would help her descend when she was ready.

"Go," Hugh said, not finishing his thought. It was too cold to leave her driver and maid standing outside, waiting. "I will stay."

With at least a little relief, Audrey left the carriage. But until he found April Barlow and the truth, neither of them would rest easy.

SIXTEEN

N oon was slipping away by the time Hugh found Stone Hollow House in the village of Wanstead. Located in a bucolic corner of Epping Forest, Wanstead Park was studded by grassy flats, marshes, islands, and ponds fed by the River Roding. A mere ten miles northwest of London, it had long drawn wealthy city dwellers to its serene pastures, Lord and Lady Gibbons among them. If his suspicion held true, he would find April Barlow here as well.

The previous night, Carrigan had slipped him into a vacant horse stall in the Violet House stables, away from the other servants. A bed of hay, a blanket, and some ale and food had restored him before he'd fallen into a shallow sleep. Just before dawn, Carrigan roused him, warning him to be gone before sun-up.

"The lad too," he'd added, and with a start, Hugh realized he wasn't alone in the stall.

Sometime during the night, Sir had found his way in and bedded down in the hay. He woke, groggy, his stomach rumbling audibly.

"Saw Bones found the lady you was looking for," he

137

announced, referring to Thornton's search for April's younger sister, who turned out be Lady Gibbons. When Sir recited the address, Carrigan had been listening; he said he'd have a mount ready for Hugh to take. *The duchess insists,* he added before Hugh could try to reject the offering. However, he wouldn't have. Getting to Wanstead efficiently and securely had, for once, trumped his pride.

Stone Hollow House was not a grandiose country estate. It was a two-story brick home, the bricks a cascade of differing buff and rose hues. The home appeared cozy and modestly refined, with bare vines climbing the exterior, and smoke billowing from the dual chimneys. Hugh stopped his borrowed mount at the head of the short drive. Other than the old painting in Sir Roberts's study, he had never laid eyes on his birth mother. Why did he feel so reluctant at the possibility of doing so now?

He dismounted and looped the reins through a brass hoop on a hitching post. There were no servants here to rush outside and take his horse, and he also felt no eyes upon him as he approached the front entrance. London was not a truly safe distance away, but at least here, he didn't feel the urge to look over his shoulder.

He brought down the knocker and only then did his pulse jump over what he might say. How he would introduce himself. When the door opened, a maid in a mob cap looked blankly upon him. Hugh cleared his throat, still deliberating if he should give his true name—if uttered as servant gossip, it might lead Bow Street officers here.

"Sir, what is your business?" the maid asked impatiently, and Hugh couldn't fault her for it. Here he stood, looking like a gaping fool.

"I am looking for Lady Gibbons."

"Is the baroness expecting you?"

"No, but it is imperative—"

"Alice?" a woman said from behind the maid. "Who is at the door?"

Then she appeared at the maid's shoulder. A woman in her late forties, with brown hair streaked with gray. Hugh recognized her from the painting. This was Lady Gibbons.

Their eyes met, and instantly, recognition smoothed her lined brow. She appeared several years younger as she stared up at Hugh, her lips parting. With misty eyes, she shooed the maid, Alice, aside and told her to fetch tea.

"Come in," Lady Gibbons said to him, waving him forward in a flustered manner. Hugh doffed his hat as he stepped into the entrance lobby.

She closed the door and turned to look upon him again, her expression a curious amalgam of excitement, sadness, and uncertainty.

"You know who I am," he said.

"I do. You look very much like your father."

Sir Robert had said the same thing. It occurred to him that a letter might have arrived from his grandfather, alerting Lady Gibbons that her sister's secret had been aired out.

"Is she here?" Hugh inquired.

He did not know which answer he wanted more. No, and he would not have to face her or her rejection of him. He should not have wanted that reply as much as he did. Lady Gibbons unknowingly chastened him when she nodded primly.

"If you will allow me a moment," she said, before then disappearing into what was most likely a drawing room. Hushed voices. The thump of something being knocked over. A chair, as his mother shot to her feet in surprise? He held his breath, listening. Wondering what she felt right then. Panic? Anger? Guilt? Hell, he had not a clue what kind of woman she was.

The kind that gave you up.

Lady Gibbons reappeared in the drawing room entrance and nodded, the signal to approach.

He'd like to have said setting eyes upon his birth mother for the first time was a momentous occasion. That he saw her, and, without warning, everything fell into place. He wanted to feel a natural connection, an instant, unexplainable bond.

Instead, he stood within the room looking upon a woman of middling height and weight, her age beginning to show upon slackened jowls and in streaks of gray in her hair. She looked every inch a school headmistress, wearing a tweed dress of muted brown, with a good amount of lace ruffle at the neck. Had they passed each other by on the street, Hugh would not have known her. He wouldn't have looked twice. April Barlow felt as unfamiliar to him as a stranger.

She looked up at him with a wavering expression, much like her sister had worn.

"You did not expect me to come," he said awkwardly. "I apologize."

She shook her head tightly. "I did expect it," she said. At his frown of confusion, she explained. "One day. I expected you one day. I always did."

A burst of frustration leaped to his tongue. "And would you have done something to bring that day about? Or would you have simply placed the responsibility into the hands of fate?"

At her stricken look, Hugh felt a prickling of guilt. Only just. Lady Gibbons clasped her hands before her and said she would go check on the tea. He barely heard her. The questions he had for Miss Barlow were so many in number they produced a din of clamor in his mind.

"Let us sit," she suggested once they were alone.

He was too restless. The idea of sitting made him feel trapped. "I would rather stand."

She nodded and remained standing as well. Hugh removed his greatcoat, which, due to Lady Gibbons's surprise at the front door, had not been taken; he now tossed it upon a chaise longue. He flexed his fingers as an unnamable irritation assailed him.

"Why?" he asked. His question, large and unwieldy as it was, needed no elaboration. She knew what he meant.

"There is much to say," she replied. Then, glimpsing at the chair behind her, the one Hugh suspected had been overturned in her surprise, she sighed. "I think I will sit."

She did, and then calmly, with a detached sort of directness, Miss Barlow began.

"I've imagined this moment countless times over the last twenty-eight years, and so I've had time to put together an answer for you. One I hoped would address all the possible questions you would have."

"One that is also truthful and not riddled with self-preserving lies, I trust," he said, refusing to feel badly for his temper.

She did not take offense, however. With a pert nod, she replied, "I think it only fair I provide you with the truth. And the truth is this: I loved you enough to realize that I did not love you enough to keep you."

Hugh stared at her, the statement slowly making sense in his mind, like a riddle and its answer coming clear.

"I see," he murmured, even though it wasn't true. She knew it.

"I don't believe you do. I will start at the beginning, and then perhaps you will. You see, my father wasn't part of London society. We were not financially sound enough to afford the life-style, and he certainly couldn't fund my coming out. So instead, my aunt offered to host me. The season turned out to be utterly unremarkable, except for one afternoon when my aunt secured us invitations to Almack's. There, I met your father for the first time. It was a brief introduction, and nothing came of it, but then, the next autumn, I met him again at a country dance near Chatham Park. He remembered me." Miss Barlow smiled wistfully. It cut into her wooden expression. Hugh suspected that to smile was unnatural for her. She spoke plainly, directly, as if instructing a classroom of her pupils.

"He was patient with me. I didn't socialize easily, and would speak directly, without artifice. It caused many others to avoid me, but Fitzgerald assured me he appreciated my candor. I knew he was a good man, and it didn't take long for us to fancy ourselves in love."

Fancy. As if now, looking back, she knew it hadn't been true.

"But as I've stated, my father was impoverished. I had no dowry to speak of, and Fitzgerald's father, the viscount, secretly had his own dwindling coffers to concern him. He required his heir to marry well, for the sake of their title and fortune. It was all very predictable, and I suppose our decision to run away together was as well. We went to Gretna Green."

The need for a seat now overtook Hugh, drowning out his restless agitation. Audrey's suggestion had been correct. He lowered himself to the edge of the chaise longue.

"You married."

"We did. Though, not over the blacksmith's anvil. No, Fitzgerald insisted on a church wedding, so we applied to Reverend McClure at the old parish church."

The sitting room's walls absorbed the confession, the enormity of it. *This* was what Eloisa had known. What Joanna, the viscountess, had known. And someone else had as well. Someone desperate to bury the secret Eloisa had exhumed.

"Then what?" he asked.

"We took rooms in a small village nearby. Fitzgerald wrote to his father, who replied straightaway with a declaration to cut off Fitzgerald altogether. There would be no money, and the viscount would not welcome us in London or anywhere else unless we annulled the marriage immediately. Fitzgerald was fond of his father, and respected the man greatly, so I knew this pained him, but he acted as though it did not. Over the next fortnight, we tried to pretend that all would be well, that we did not need the viscount's money or acceptance. But I knew the truth. I saw the regret in my husband's eyes nearly constantly. We'd acted rashly, and he *wanted* to annul."

"Did you go through with it?" A flicker of hope warmed Hugh. But she shook her head.

"You must know that Fitzgerald was far too good a man, too loyal and gallant. No, he decided to go to London to speak with his father. Convince him of the marriage. Before he left Scotland, I told him I would agree to an annulment. They are difficult to obtain, but I thought that it might be best. He grew angry and defensive. He couldn't admit he'd made a mistake."

"Or perhaps he loved you and didn't want to annul, as you suspected."

Miss Barlow sealed her lips against an instant retort. The sitting room went quiet. The whole house seemed to be so. Neither Lady Gibbons or her maid had returned with tea, and Hugh knew it was purposeful. They were being given privacy.

"I do think he cared for me," she said after a moment. "But enough to withstand the weight of the challenges against us? No. And in truth, my love for him was equally impressionable."

She spoke with nearly no emotion. These were all simple facts to her, past events that she had come to terms with, had lived with, for nearly three decades now, while Hugh sat across from her, struggling with them, much like a landed fish, gasping for breath.

"He left for London, and shortly after, I left the rooms we'd let together. I thought it would be best to disappear, in turn relieving him of the decision he could not, and would not, make."

Had he returned to Scotland, only to find empty rooms? His wife gone? Hugh felt a strike of pity for his dead father and what he must have gone through.

"Where did you go?" he asked, keeping to himself his low opinion of her choice.

"My late mother had a cousin in Wales. She agreed to my stay, and when, shortly after my arrival, I realized I was with child, she kindly did not turn me out."

Hugh lowered his head, suddenly weary. He rubbed the back of his neck, the muscles there corded with tension. "You did not send word to him."

"No. I wanted him to return to his life in London and forget me. If he knew of my condition, he would never have been able to do that."

"You made all the decisions for him, it seems. How benevolent of you." Hugh shot to his feet and stalked to the window. Outside, a fine freezing rain fell.

That his father might have wanted to remain married to her, that he might have loved her more than he feared the burdens of his father's displeasure, had not even occurred to her? How dare she strip him of those choices?

"Are you angry? I anticipated that you might be," she said, still seated in her chair.

Hugh turned back to face her, astounded. Did she truly not know? The searching look upon her face gave him an answer.

"It doesn't matter," he said. "There are important things I need to know."

"Such as?"

"Did my father annul the marriage in your absence before he married Joanna?"

With the solemn shake of her head, Hugh's world began to

crumble. A chiming in his ears joined with Miss Barlow's voice as she explained.

"My sister has always been my confidant, and after four months away, I decided I could bear it no longer. I sent word to her, asking her to keep my whereabouts secret. She was ecstatic to hear from me, and furious as well. It seems my father and Fitzgerald's covered up our elopement so well that there was no scandal, no whispers at all in regard to our trip to Gretna Green. Fitzgerald had apparently traveled to France to sow his wild oats, while I went off to care for my mother's sick cousin in Wales. Imagine! I had been hiding right where they'd lied about my being."

"Go on," Hugh said, impatient.

She did not bristle as any other woman might have when being given such a brusque command. In fact, she seemed not to hear his tone of voice at all.

"My sister informed me that the viscount had died, quite suddenly, some months before. And that Fitzgerald, the new Viscount Neatham, had posted marriage banns to Miss Joanna Paulson."

Audrey's supposition that it had taken a matter of months —one winter season—for all of this to unfurl had been spot on. For him to have proposed marriage to Joanna, Hugh's father had to have believed April Barlow was lost to him forever.

"Why didn't you go to him?" Hugh asked, flummoxed. "The man opposing your marriage had died."

"Yes, but nothing had changed. Fitzgerald still needed to marry well, now more than before. His estate was in shambles. Joanna's dowry would save it. And besides, after some months apart, I realized I didn't want to be his wife any longer."

And she didn't appear to feel a lick of remorse about it, either.

"What *were* your plans then, because I cannot fathom what

was going through your head," he said, honestly and utterly confounded. "You were with child, hiding out in Wales. You were going to allow your husband to marry another woman, who, by the way, was walking into a marriage that she did not know was invalid. I have no love the woman, but she was duped and for that I feel pity for her."

Miss Barlow sat still, gazing up at him with a placid expression. The notion came to him that perhaps this was no act. Miss Barlow could, in all actuality, be a woman of little feeling and compassion.

"I planned to have you, and I did, in late November. I planned to raise you at my cousin's home, and she and her husband were willing to take us on as wards. However, after a few months of motherhood, I began to comprehend that I lacked a certain...attitude that I'd witnessed in other mothers. I felt no ill will toward you. I felt mild affection, but I knew enough to know that was no way to feel for my own child."

It was a painfully honest statement, and Hugh felt it like a clamping vise around his heart.

"I went to London and arranged for a meeting with Fitzgerald. He was furious. I'd hurt him terribly by running away. He sent a private detective to search for me but then, his father died, and he was faced with the estate's insufficient funds. He let me go, and moved on with his life, as if he had never married."

To let all and sundry know that he had wed Miss Barlow, but she had run off on him, would have been a damaging blow to his reputation. Applying for an annulment would have made him a social pariah, which would also stamp out any possibility of saving the estate through a beneficial marriage. Hugh couldn't fault his father for his choices.

"He was married and expecting his first child," she continued. "It was quite a blow to him, to realize he already had an heir. There was nothing to be done about it, however. To come forward with the truth would ruin him. It would ruin Joanna, and their child would be ruined even before birth. The potential scandal was too great. We agreed that the only way forward was for him to raise you as a ward. You would be given a gentleman's upbringing and he would provide you with a living once you came of age."

And being the good man that he was, his father had stood by his word. He'd arranged for a kind and loving woman to mother him, he had given him the same education he did his other children, and he had endured not only the whispers and admonishments made behind his back but the slow decay of his marriage to Joanna due to his actions. Due to his devotion to his son. His heir.

Fucking hell.

Hugh was the true heir to the Neatham viscountcy.

Barty, Eloisa, Thomas...*they* were illegitimate.

"Someone else knows the truth," he said, his mind fleeing from the distant past and toward more recent events. "Eloisa Neatham heard your name many years ago on her mother's lips. She insinuated that Barty was not heir. Last week, Eloisa asked me to track you down and get the truth, perhaps proof, and she was murdered for it."

At this, Miss Barlow did shift her expression. Interest and alarm brightened her eyes.

"I read in the papers that she was killed. And that you were wanted in connection. But I did not know that she was searching for me."

"Who was the man who warned you off at your school?" he asked.

"How do you know of that?"

"I just do," he said, unwilling to explain his every move. "And I believe he is connected to the murder."

Hugh's tension subsided somewhat. This was more familiar ground. Investigating, asking questions, and attempting to piece together answers all brought Hugh's reeling head to a standstill.

Miss Barlow canted her head. "I don't see how. The man you speak of had nothing to do with Lady Eloisa. He gave no name, though he was quality, I can tell you that. He warned me to reject Mrs. Susan Smith's application for her daughter to attend my school. I had not yet even met with the woman; her letter of introduction and interest had barely been received when this man appeared late at night at the school with his threats."

"What threats?"

"That if I didn't heed his command, Mrs. Smith and I would both find ourselves at the bottom of the Thames," she answered coolly, as though not at all unnerved.

"You mean to say he mentioned nothing about the Neatham heir, or your secret marriage?"

She shook her head. "But it did worry me. I thought it best to stay away from the school for a short while, and I instructed my assistant to tell Mrs. Smith, who was due to visit the school, that there was no room for placement."

Susan Smith. When Miss Carey had mentioned her, Hugh had deduced that was the *nom de guerre* Eloisa had used to gain entry at the school. The excuse that she wanted to place her daughter there had been a ploy.

Hugh looked again out the window. Rain was still falling, driving at a sideways clip. It was an hour's ride back to London; he would be soaked through when he returned. He could go to Thornton's clinic and use the key that he still had in his pocket. But first, he'd have to find a way to return Audrey's horse.

"You are a Bow Street officer," Miss Barlow stated. "You are gathering information to help your case, I presume."

"Yes," he said.

"And you are running from those whom you would normally call colleagues."

Though she likely didn't intend for it, the observation cut to the quick. Miss Barlow hadn't an ounce of delicacy. Hugh at met other people like her before; odd sorts, unable to converse or act appropriately when with others. He suspected that this trait of hers had led her to make the decisions she had. And he found that although he wished to be angry with her, he couldn't.

Hugh went to the chaise longue and retrieved his hat and greatcoat. "I will take my leave."

"You can stay here. My sister and her husband will offer you shelter."

"No," he said, and though he meant to follow up with a reason why, his tongue fell useless. He shook his head and started for the sitting room entranceway. It had all been such a disappointment. This meeting, Miss Barlow's story, the lack of a connection to the man who'd taken the folio. Hugh drew back a moment at the thought of official papers.

"Is there proof of the marriage? A certificate?" he asked. If one existed, whoever possessed it could be in danger.

"I have it at my school, among my things. I thought of destroying it a number of times, but there was always something that stopped me." She frowned, and Hugh thought he saw a glimmer of remorse. Or perhaps it was only calculation; the certificate held some value and she had known it. However, the man who'd threatened her had not been aware at all.

"I will return to Field Street and have the certificate delivered to you," Miss Barlow said.

"No, do not leave Wanstead for now. It is safer to keep your distance from that certificate," he said. "I'll send word here when you can return to your school. It is enough for now to know that you have it."

"You wish to prove you are heir?" she asked.

Hugh bristled. "No. What I want is to prove I had no motive to silence Eloisa." Her killer wanted the truth hushed up, and that pointed to someone tied to the current holders of the Neatham title.

Barty? Thomas? Thomas had been at Lady Reed's the next morning. Audrey had spoken to him. Hugh wanted to speak to him as well, but as he was currently a fugitive from the law, showing his face anywhere would be too dangerous.

He said good day to Miss Barlow and again, turned to leave. However, he paused. Though this time, he did not look back at her when he spoke.

"I thank you," he said, surely startling her as much as he did himself. "When you made the choice to give me to my father, he asked a woman who had never married but always wanted a child to raise me. Her name was Catherine Marsden. I thought you should know that she didn't just raise me. She loved me. And I loved her, as a son loves his mother."

Hugh swallowed the lump in his throat and left the room. There was nothing more to say.

CHAPTER
SEVENTEEN

Despite Philip recently reminding her of it, Audrey had completely forgotten about the military review in Hyde Park that they were to attend with Michael, Genie, and Cassie. When the three of them arrived at Violet House, all turned out in fashionably warm clothes suitable for the military spectacle, Audrey had flushed with embarrassment. To make matters worse, Philip had *not* forgotten. He appeared in the entrance hall with his velvet-lined greatcoat, top hat, and yellow buckskin gloves, prepared to leave as they had all planned two weeks previously.

"You could have reminded me again," she said to him churlishly after pulling him aside on her way to her bedchamber to quickly dress with Greer.

"I have been preoccupied," he replied with a meaningful stare. With Freddie Walker. Of course. And she had been preoccupied with Hugh. Though, Philip didn't know that. Then, it struck her: What did he imagine she had been up to since the murder of Lady Eloisa? Did he truly believe she was doing nothing to help Hugh? With a start, she realized that he hadn't inquired at all.

Because he is preoccupied.

Without another word, she'd gone to her room to find something appropriate to wear. Like a magician, Greer had already been in the boudoir, selecting an ensemble.

As she'd dressed, she thought of Hugh. Carrigan whispered that he'd gone to Wanstead, and she imagined that was where Miss Barlow's sister lived. He'd be gone most of the day. But if a highway patrolman came upon him along the road toward Wanstead and South Woodford...she worried he'd be caught.

But he was resourceful. Audrey knew she had to trust in his ability to get himself out of any sticky situation. She'd put her worries aside and finished dressing in the dark blue promenade grown embroidered with gold damask that Greer selected. The skirt was lined to block the wind, and a matching blue pelisse with gold piping would help keep her warm.

They arrived at Hyde Park later than they'd wanted, missing the Horse Guard parade entirely and arriving in the middle of the mock skirmish; scores of fired blank cartridges had created drifting clouds of gunpowder smoke that stung their eyes. Michael graciously pretended not to be put out, but as he and Philip left the ladies to view what was left of the skirmish, Audrey knew he was. Having been in the army as an officer, Michael enjoyed these reviews. Philip went out of duty to his brother, though he didn't pretend at interest, and Michael knew better than to expect it. Usually, Audrey and Genie enjoyed observing the younger ladies flirting with the men in uniform.

They'd anticipated Cassie being such a young lady, but as they walked along the banks of the Serpentine, gloved hands warmly tucked into ermine muffs, Philip's sister barely said a word. The previous evening at Genie's ball, she'd seemed happier, especially after being the only young lady whom Mr. William Knowlton could manage to pay attention to. No longer, it seemed.

"I much prefer the summer reviews," Genie said as the percussion of drums rolled through the park. The tip of her nose was red, and she looked like she would have happily crawled into her ermine muff if she would have fit.

"This smoke is wretched," Audrey commented, and with an eye on the slate clouds coming in overhead, added, "And there is to be rain."

A pavilion had been erected for the festivities, and as she looked toward it now, noticed a familiar face. "Perhaps we should move to the pavilion," Audrey said, reaching over to pinch Cassie's sleeve. "If I'm not mistaken, that is William."

Genie's brother diverted his attention from those he stood with and peered in their direction. It seemed he had spied them already before they had him. He smiled shyly, and Cassie went still in her tracks.

"Oh, no," she murmured.

Audrey stepped in front of her, hoping to obscure her sudden expression of dread from William. "What is the matter? You were giddy over him last evening, were you not?"

"My brother did not offend you in any way, I hope?" Genie asked, joining Audrey in forming a shield around Cassie. William would see their backs, not the young woman's quickly paling face.

"Not at all, no," she replied, sounding breathless. She raised her ermine muff so high she nearly concealed her face with it. Had her hands been free she might have sealed her palms to her cheeks. "Mr. Knowlton is a perfect gentleman. I don't think I've met anyone so amiable before. And he is the only man I've met who has read and enjoyed Mrs. Radcliffe's novels! I think he might have enjoyed *The Mysteries of Udolpho* more than I."

Audrey pinned her lower lip against a grin. This bubbly side of Cassie was one she missed a great deal. It was clear she took an interest in William.

"Then why does the thought of seeing him here make you look so miserable? I half think you'll need smelling salts in a moment," Genie replied.

Cassie turned on her heel and began to walk in the direction they'd come. "Because I *am* miserable. I think he is wonderful."

Audrey and Genie hurried after her.

"Then what is the problem?" Audrey asked. "He is quite obviously taken with you."

"He shouldn't be," she said, and the true reason for Cassie's odd reaction became evident. She doubted herself.

"I am a fraud. He believes me an innocent debutante, and I am not," she said, whispering so low Audrey barely heard the confession under all the military drumming. "Am I to lie to him?"

Genie parted her lips to reply, but then sealed them again. Apparently, she didn't know how to reply any better than Audrey. Lying to William would be wrong; telling him the truth would cause even the kindest suitor to bid her farewell.

"I think you should enjoy William's attention," Genie said after some hesitation.

"It doesn't have to be more complicated than that right now," Audrey agreed. "He hasn't declared himself."

But she worried, the way William had gazed upon Cassie the evening before, and just now, from the pavilion, that an offer would be forthcoming.

"I suppose you are right," Cassie said, though she didn't sound certain. "I just don't want to grow too fond of him if it is all for naught."

Genie stopped her with a hand to her forearm. "He saw us just now. Let me go tell him you dropped your glove and turned to look for it. Come to the pavilion when you're ready."

Audrey marveled at her sister-in-law's tact and grace. Of

course, she wouldn't want her brother to think Cassie was fleeing from him.

"Let's find your glove," Audrey said with a wry glance at Cassie. A hint of a grin broke over her lips as they ambled a little further along.

Now that they were alone, an opportunity arose for a conversation Audrey had been avoiding.

"I must apologize to you, Cassie. I feel responsible for your decision to leave Violet House for Michael and Genie's."

She drew short and peered at Audrey. "Responsible how?"

"Because I found yet another dead body," she said with a wave of her hand, as if it should be obvious. "I am starting to believe I'm cursed."

To this, Cassie surprised her and laughed. A full-throated chuckle that caused a passing couple to crane their necks and stare.

"You are not cursed," she said. "I don't believe in such stuff and nonsense. But I admit, I left rather poorly. I should be the one apologizing. I was being selfish."

Audrey stopped her and with a raised finger, crouched, as if to grab a lost glove. Standing again, she shook her head. "Selfish how?"

They turned and started toward the pavilion again. "I feared more scrutiny. Finding a dead woman would certainly bring it to your door, and lately, I seem to live in fear. I don't want anyone to find out the truth, Audrey. I don't think I could bear the humiliation."

There was nothing she could say to Philip's sister to convince her that threat didn't exist. Because it did. So instead, she peeled one hand from her muff and wrapped her arm around Cassie's shoulder. They walked several steps in silence.

"Have you heard anything from Officer Marsden?" Cassie asked after a prolonged stretch. Audrey released her and stuck her cold hand back into the impossibly soft muff. It was little comfort.

"No." She hated lying to Cassie, especially since she was opening up to Audrey for the first time in months.

"He is no murderer," Cassie said. She had met Hugh the previous summer and had been fascinated by him.

"No, he is not." Audrey then held her tongue. It wasn't that she didn't trust Cassie...with anything else she might have confided in her. But not this. Not with Hugh's very life on the line. It would only take one slip of the tongue, one gaff, and everything could come tumbling down.

They reached the pavilion and slipped under the pitched roof. With the threatening clouds, a few dozen or more people had gathered there. Past top hats and bonnets, through capes and pelisses, Audrey's eyes spotted Lady Redding—otherwise known as Millie. Her older sister.

She stood among a pack of other ladies giving their attention to three red-coated military men. Their uniforms were of crisp wool, bright crimson and spotless white, adorned with braids, tassels, shining gold buttons and ribbons denoting their rank, of which Audrey was entirely ignorant. However, one of the soldiers was none other than Colonel Trenton, Eloisa's brother. His attention grazed over Audrey and upon recognizing her, dipped his head into an almost imperceptible bow while the others around him still conversed.

Millie, a widow for four years now, had either pinched her cheeks to bring color to them, or she was actually blushing as she listened to the soldiers giving them their favor. Nearly ten years Audrey's senior, Millie had married a viscount of advanced age when Audrey had been nine. She and her sister had never been close, and understandably so. Millie was just so much older. She was also a good bit like their mother, the baroness. Cold, distant, and extremely caring of her position within society's good graces. On the other hand, James, Audrey's brother, had been six years her senior and had still doted on his little imp of a sister. He'd taken after their father, who showered Audrey with affection as well. Losing them both to a fever shortly after Millie's marriage had devastated her. She'd been left alone at Haverfield with her cold mother and her uncle, the new baron, and they did not hide their romantic affair very well, even during the time the baroness should have been in mourning.

Millie's circle of friends and acquaintances differed from Audrey's, and that was just fine by her. Her sister's presence tended to result in tensed shoulders and agitation that would linger for hours afterward, where Audrey went over everything they had said to one another, every action, with a fine-toothed comb in her mind.

She tried to tuck herself behind Genie in the hope that she would remain unseen. Speaking to Colonel Trenton again might only bring up the murder, and Cassie had already conveyed worry over the attention. But when William bowed at the hip and greeted her with an all too jovial "Your Grace, it is a pleasure," his voice carried.

Millie's sharp brown eyes sliced toward her. Audrey met her with a thin smile, though Millie didn't return it right away. She seemed to hesitate, wavering over whether to excuse herself and come say hello. Suspecting that Millie might admonish her for hesitating, and then accusing her of being high in the instep, Audrey made the first move. She excused herself from Cassie, Genie, and William, and crossed the pavilion. Millie saw her approaching and hitched her chin, putting on a false smile.

"You Grace," she said with a small dip of her head, the public show of respect not something she would have done in private.

"Lady Redding, I hope you're enjoying the review." Calling

her Millie in public would have been too informal and something her sister would lambast her for later.

Her group of ladies and officers waited for an introduction, and Millie dutifully—if grudgingly—obliged. She ran through the names of the ladies and officers. Colonel Trenton refrained from speaking. Saying anything about their previous encounter at Lady Reed's, now that the marchioness was so recently deceased, would have instantly consumed the light conversation. And though the others surely connected Audrey to the discovery of Colonel Trenton's recently murdered sister, that topic was also not broached. Instead, Audrey settled for a superficial compliment.

"My felicitations, Colonel, I hear you are to be wed."

The colonel, his expression flat, gave another bow. "I am, Your Grace. Thank you."

At the drop of silence afterward, and Millie's stricken glare, Audrey wondered if perhaps offering congratulations rather than condolences had been a gaff. Explaining that she had already met with the colonel and conveyed her sympathies earlier would have left her sounding like a babbling fool.

Another officer came to her rescue. He clicked his heels and bowed. "Captain Marcott of the 29th Regiment of Foot, at your service, Your Grace. I am acquainted with Lord Herrick. We were in the Peninsula together."

"A pleasure to meet you," Audrey said. "I arrived with his lordship just now. He is here, somewhere. I hope you will meet with him."

It was a mundane comment, but Audrey didn't wish to be drawn into any conversation. Her intent was to say hello and then excuse herself. Surely, that was all Millie wished for too.

Captain Marcott bowed again, graciously, his gloved hand resting on the ornate gold hilt of his short sword. All the officers and infantrymen were kitted out in full ceremonial dress, and that included the short sword. Next to his impeccably white glove, the sidearm's decorative tassel—crimson to match the uniform—stood in stark contrast. Her attention caught and held on the tassel.

"Your sword, Captain," Audrey said before she could stop to think.

Captain Marcott looked down at it. "Yes, Your Grace, I know it is rather boorish to wear such a weapon in the presence of ladies. If it were up to me, we would leave them off. This isn't Waterloo, after all, now is it?"

There was a polite round of twittering laughs at his quip, however as Audrey's eyes shifted toward Colonel Trenton, saw that he was not joining in. His eyes were no longer red-rimmed as they had been the morning after the disastrous soiree, but he still appeared melancholy.

Audrey looked back to Captain Marcott and his sword hilt and tassel. A strip of black leather tied the tassel to the gold hilt, the leather strip itself pinned together in the center by a gold leaf charm. Below the charm, the red tassel swung freely. She blinked. That charm. She recognized it.

"Captain, do all dress swords have that tassel and gold leaf charm?" she asked.

The question was met with a glare from Millie. She supposed it was an odd inquiry, but that charm was the very replica of the one she had trod upon in Lady Reed's ballroom while running through, in search of the woman who had screamed. Its design, three leaves fanned out, was unmistakable. The short, sharp post that had pierced the sole of her slipper and her foot would have been the length needed to pin the tassel's leather strips too.

Without any hint of amusement, Officer Marcott answered, "Yes, Your Grace. Is it not to your liking? I admit, the ornamentation is a bit ostentatious."

"I am sure my sister does not mean any insult," Millie said quickly, her smile showing too much tooth. Audrey knew that look; it was the one that implored her to hush up. Audrey was embarrassing her, surely.

"None at all, officer. I was simply curious, as I believe I have seen it before," Audrey said.

A military man had been at Lady Reed's ball, it seemed. She didn't recall seeing one there, however. They stood out in a crowd, what with the vibrant red uniform and their tall, feathered shako caps. However, she *had* seen a military man at Lady Reed's the following day.

As gracefully and indifferently as possible, Audrey turned her attention toward Colonel Trenton. He was in possession of a short sidearm, just as all the other military men were, however his gloved hand rested upon the hilt, obscuring the tassel and charm.

"Of course, you have seen it before, my dear," Millie said with a silly twittering laugh. "We are surrounded by them today. Officers, I hope we aren't keeping you from your drills."

She wanted to move away from Audrey's strange question, and Colonel Trenton seemed to be of the same inclination. He bowed in a clipped manner and was the first to take his leave from the group. Millie noticed and glowered at Audrey, surely blaming her for driving away the colonel. Audrey ignored her, following Colonel Trenton's movement as he left the pavilion, his hand still covering his hilt and tassel. Her mind churned.

Like Bartholomew, Colonel Trenton would be ruined if Hugh's father and April Barlow wed at Gretna Green, unbeknownst to anyone else. His legitimacy would be negated. She recollected again the colonel's red, puffy eyes when crossing paths with him at Lady Reed's. She had thought the state of his eyes was due to sobbing over his sister's death. His hoarse voice, evidence as well.

But hadn't she, Philip, and Cassie complained of sore throats the next morning? Her eyes had stung something wicked, and Greer had whipped up a compress to help reduce the inflammation. They had watered incessantly too. All because of the caustic smoke.

Captain Marcott and the remaining officer bowed and departed next, and Millie pressed her lips thinly. "So good to see you, as always, sister," she said with barely concealed rancor before she and her friends carried onward, toward another part of the pavilion.

She ignored Millie and turned back toward Genie and Cassie. The pavilion had thickened with crowds as a fine mist began to fall. Cassie was locked in a pleasant conversation with William and a few others when Audrey drew Genie aside.

"I must leave," she blurted, to which Genie's grin crashed.

"What is wrong? Did Lady Redding say something unpleasant to you? Should we find Philip and Michael?" She began to look about, in search of them.

"It is just a head ache," Audrey lied. "I will send Carrigan back after he leaves me at Violet House."

That wasn't where she was going, of course. What she wanted was to find Hugh and tell him what she might have just discovered. But he would currently be in Wanstead. Who knew when he would be returning? Or if he would even come to see her after.

"Oh, there they are," Genie said, her search stopping as she found Philip and Michael standing along the edge of Rotten Row. "Let us fetch Philip."

"No." Audrey clamped her hand on Genie's forearm in a startling and ungainly fashion. She jumped, and her eyes narrowed with alarm.

"No, that isn't necessary," Audrey went on, releasing the claw-like grip on her sister-in-law. Her stomach turned leaden as she saw that Philip and Michael did not stand alone. A handful of other men stood with them. Mr. Freddie Walker included.

Right then, Philip felt so far away from her that she couldn't even begin to imagine traversing the gap.

"Stay. Enjoy yourselves. And keep an eye on Cassie," she added, then turned and started toward the closest park gate.

Hugh had spoken of not being able to go to Sir Gabriel until he had proof in his hand. If only she had kept the charm and not tossed it away! But she could amend her witness testimony. She could appeal to Officer Tyne and draw connections to the gold leaf charm's presence and Colonel Trenton's appearance the next morning. Could it be enough to warrant Officer Tyne questioning him of his whereabouts that evening? Maybe. Maybe not. But she had to try.

"Your Grace," Carrigan said as she came upon the coach. He looked for the others in her party and when he didn't see them, returned his attention to her. "Are we going somewhere, Your Grace?"

"Yes," she said as he lowered the step and extended his hand. "To Bow Street. Quick."

CHAPTER
EIGHTEEN

Sir Gabriel Poston's residence wasn't far from Bow Street. The work-obsessed knight and his wife lived a few blocks away, on Tavistock, which ran parallel to the Strand. Several fashionable shops lined Tavistock Street, and during the daylight hours, carriages and their teams cluttered up the road in an equally maddening and impressive manner. It made one think that to pass by Tavistock without popping in would be a mistake, and its shops rivaled those of Bond and Oxford Streets.

An icy crust had formed on Hugh's greatcoat by the time he crossed into the city just before nightfall. He'd spent the ride from Wanstead mulling over everything Miss Barlow had divulged. Going over it again and again seemed to harden him to it, much like the crust of ice on his coat. There was no room for emotions, not right now. Later, he could wallow and rage, but now, he could only have one objective: prove his innocence by finding Eloisa's murderer.

It was a risk, but as he neared the city, its skyline swelling with every stride of his borrowed horse, Hugh decided there was only one person who could assist him in an official capacity. One person who stood between Hugh and the gallows. He had taken a chance on Hugh before, when all polite society had shunned and maligned him.

He approached Tavistock Street from the far western end, away from Bow Street. Since it was past dark, most shops had closed, and carriages were at a minimum. Going to the magistrate's offices was out of the question. However, if Sir Gabriel was at home without company, Hugh might be able to get away with a surreptitious meeting. Rebecca, Lady Poston and certainly Sir Gabriel's better half, had always adored Hugh, and he could only hope she did not believe the rumors.

While it wasn't proof, April Barlow's confession offered strong motive for Bartholomew to silence his sister and stop her crusade to ruin him. Eloisa had despised her brother for sending her away, for exiling her from London and treating her as if she was the one to blame for what happened. She had no choice but to defer to Barty, who was the viscount and eldest brother. Thomas had to defer to him too. But Thomas had not paid for his part in the debacle, had he? He had merely been ordered to join the royal army and make something of himself. Eloisa's bitter fury was not unwarranted.

Hugh dismounted and left Fournier's horse tied off at the curb. He hoped to hell no thief wandered by and scarpered off with it. The windows of Sir Gabriel's home were lit, emitting a welcome glow. Hugh shivered. He would take his chances.

After a few raps of the knocker, a servant opened the door.

"Good evening, madam. Officer Tyne to see Sir Gabriel, if he is not already entertaining other guests."

The lie would only work if Tyne had never come by the residence and made himself known to the maid, and the gamble paid off. She allowed Hugh into the foyer, her eyes taking in the state of his coat and hat, and then bustled off to announce him.

The foyer exuded understated elegance. A single vase of flowers centered a small round table underneath a silver framed beveled mirror. Maroon carpet ran the stairs, an oil landscape in vivid golds, oranges, and blues displayed talent, and an alabaster bust of Themis, the goddess of justice, blindfolded and holding a balancing scale aloft, flaunted Sir Gabriel's passion and purpose.

If he did not give Hugh aid tonight, he would at least give him a ten-minute advantage to disappear into London again.

The maid reappeared and on her heels was the barrel-chested chief magistrate, in his shirtsleeves and waistcoat. His thunderous expression at the notion that Tyne had come to his residence changed first to surprise, then to exasperation when he saw Hugh standing in his front hall. Sir Gabriel thinned his lips and spared the maid a furtive glance before clearing his throat. "Officer Tyne. My study. Now."

Hopes lifting, Hugh followed his swift strides down the narrow hall off the foyer. The magistrate had concealed Hugh's identity to prevent his servant from rushing to the backrooms and telling the other staff. That might mean he wanted to help. However, when Sir Gabriel closed the study door behind him and turned to face Hugh, the man was practically fulminating.

"God damn it, Marsden, where in Hades's bollocks have you been? I have men turning this city inside out searching for you, and you waltz into my home looking like a drowned river rat? I want answers, and I want them right now."

Had he been standing in Sir Gabriel's office at Bow Street fielding the man's ire, Hugh would have been gritting his molars and devising a way to extricate himself from the room. However now, after the last few hellish days, the magistrate's booming voice was a familiar balm.

"I've been trying not to get arrested and hanged for a murder I didn't commit," Hugh replied as he peeled off his greatcoat, hat, and gloves. Sir Gabriel went to a table crammed with glass decanters and poured them both generous splashes of whisky.

"Hell, I know you didn't do it," he said, "but you made yourself look goddamn guilty disappearing like that. Not to mention your history with Neatham, your behavior at his home, and the past rumors regarding the lady. None of it is in your favor. In fact, you would have been wiser to hop a packet to Calais."

He handed Hugh the cut crystal snifter. Hugh gripped its curved base, staring at the magistrate in disbelief. He didn't know if Sir Gabriel's suggestion amused or frightened him.

"Do you have no other suspects?" Hugh asked.

"Of course not," he growled. "The viscount is determined to pin this on you, and your assault against him hours before his sister was killed hasn't helped you, Marsden. He is convinced it was an act of revenge. Said you'd come to his home, spouting off about Eloisa being in London and coming to see you. That you were frothing at the bit over some secret she was keeping from you. He says you went mad, leapt across his bloody desk, and attacked him!"

Hugh downed the whisky. "That last part is true. And Eloisa did come to see me a few days before her murder with a secret. You might want to sit down. It's a long story."

"No need." Sir Gabriel was already pouring himself another whisky. "I've already heard it."

Hugh's grip on his empty glass slackened. "What? How?"

"Your duchess. She came to see me earlier this afternoon."

Audrey. His pulse quickened as possible reasons why she would go to the chief magistrate streamed through his mind. What had happened since he'd left town that morning?

"I know about April Barlow and the theory that perhaps she and your father married, that you were born before

Bartholomew, and that you could be heir, not him," he summarized as he lowered himself into a chair adjacent the hearth. A fire warmed Hugh as he took the chair opposite.

"It's no longer mere theory. I've just come from a meeting with Miss Barlow. The marriage was done in Scotland, at the old parish church in Gretna Green. My father's father was hoping for an annulment, so he concealed the truth to stave off scandal. But then he died, and my father was in dire straits. He was in debt up to his ears, and Miss Barlow had run off with no word, no indication of where she'd gone. My father thought all evidence of his elopement had vanished, and to save the estate, he married again, this time prosperously. Only...he didn't know Miss Barlow was with child."

"Bloody Christ." The magistrate sank back into his chair. It seemed an appropriate reaction.

"She asked my father to care for me when she...decided that it was too much for her," Hugh said succinctly, without the bitter tang of the truer words: *abandoned him.*

"And where did Miss Barlow go from there?"

"She started a finishing school for young ladies. In fact, Eloisa learned that Miss Barlow was missing from her finishing school—"

"How?" Sir Gabriel interjected.

"She'd gone there and been told that the headmistress had disappeared."

The magistrate grumbled, a sound he made when skeptical. "How would Eloisa have known to go there? How did she find this April Barlow woman in the first place?"

Hugh had wondered that as well. How had she known? Eloisa had also said that until recently, she had not given thought to the name April Barlow. How then had she so recently come upon the name again?

The magistrate's study seemed to disappear all around him as Hugh's muddled mind cleared. Eloisa had spent all these years hiding in the countryside, while Lady Cassandra, the duke's sister, had returned after a handful of months away, having birthed her child in secret. Cassie, devastated over having to give up her child and return. Eloisa, whose baby had died. Why then stay away? Why not return?

"Miss Susan Smith," Hugh whispered.

Sir Gabriel turned his ear. "Come again?"

Hugh got to his feet, blood beginning to pump hard. Christ, he'd been daft. "Eloisa gave Miss Carey, the assistant head-mistress at the school, a pseudonym, claiming that she wanted to place her daughter at the school. I thought it was a ruse, a cover for Eloisa to gain access to April Barlow..."

He couldn't stand still. Hugh paced to the magistrate's desk and back again.

"It wasn't a ruse. That's how she heard Miss Barlow's name again. When she'd looked into the school, in earnest. For her daughter."

A child that had not been stillborn, as Eloisa claimed. She'd raised the child in the country. That was why Barty had forbidden her to come back to London. Because Eloisa had refused to give up her daughter. Barty had lied. He'd known the child hadn't died.

Sir Gabriel sat forward in his seat. "Lady Eloisa has a child? Does she have a husband?"

Hugh sealed his lips, belatedly recalling his company. Eloisa's condition had never been made known. To anyone familiar with the scandal, she had only left London in shame for having been ruined by her own half-brother. Not that she had found herself increasing.

Even now, Hugh found his tongue growing leaden as he

avoided discussing the unsavory truth. He had not shared it with anyone, ever. Not even Thornton. In fact, it seemed that whenever his mind even so much as approached the memories from those wretched few days, six years ago, it would immediately reject them. He would veer in any direction but the direction of the truth.

"Why was the duchess here?" Hugh asked, again avoiding. He faced the magistrate. "You never said. Why did she come?"

Sir Gabriel was no fool. He knew his question was being circumnavigated. But he acquiesced. "She wants me to question Colonel Trenton."

Hugh grimaced. "Thomas? Why?"

What had Audrey discovered? Hell, he hated that they needed to work apart. He'd been cut off from her, and he felt the breach keenly.

"At the ball where Eloisa was killed, she was running through the smoky brume when she trod upon a gold leaf charm. It pierced her slipper and her foot, but she tossed it aside after removing it. Today, at the military review in Hyde Park, she learned the same gold leaf charm is affixed to every officer's dress sidearm."

"Including Colonel Trenton's," Hugh said, understanding.

"Indeed. He was not at the ball, however. I've had the guest list from Lord Reed."

"No, but the following morning—"

"Yes, yes, she told me about seeing him at Lady Reed's. His puffy eyes and reddened skin, his hoarse voice...all which could be attributed to a brother's grief," Sir Gabriel said.

"Or exposure to a caustic smoke bomb." Hugh ran a hand through his hair; the strands were damp, the late winter rain having utterly soaked his hat through. Shivers gripped his body, tensing his muscles.

"He has motive," Hugh said. "Both Trenton and Neatham. If

they knew their parents' marriage was null and void, if they knew they were illegitimate—"

"If they knew you were the true heir," the magistrate inserted, assuring Hugh he was with him in his line of thought. "I need proof of it."

"Miss Barlow has the certificate of marriage among her things at the Field Street school. And surely there will be record of the marriage in Reverend McClure's register at the parish church," Hugh said.

"I've already sent a man on the Great North Road to Gretna Green with instruction to check the records at the blacksmith's as well as the churches. After Her Grace's visit, I thought it would be prudent," Sir Gabriel replied. "I will send another officer to Field Street to find that certificate."

In a day already brimming with surprises, this one nearly overwhelmed Hugh. "You will?"

"Of course. I want that record. I want proof you are heir, which would give a motive for Neatham or Trenton to have wanted to silence their sister."

Sir Gabriel was on his side. Hugh should have known he would be. The knight was a brusque and no-nonsense sort of man who could rip you to shreds with a set down before sending you out the door again with a pat on your back.

"What I don't understand, however," he went on, "is why Lady Eloisa would wish to ruin her brothers so thoroughly. Why loathe them so much that she would also expose her own illegitimacy just to see them destroyed?"

Hugh walked to the hearth and held his palms to the flames. He wasn't yet ready to give up that piece of the puzzle; as usual, even the thought of telling Sir Gabriel made his lips seal tighter.

"I will speak to Tyne—the *real* Tyne," the magistrate added with a groan, "and have him speak to Colonel Trenton about that night. See where he was at the time. What we've discussed here, about April Barlow, will stay between us. *For now.*"

He stressed the last bit. Meaning there might soon come a time when it would be made known. When his legitimate birth was exposed to the House of Lords. When he would be declared heir.

"I don't want it," he said. "I don't care about the title. I just want Eloisa's murderer found. I want my life back."

The magistrate made no comment. Likely because he didn't believe the claim. Who in their rational mind wouldn't want to titled and heir to a wealthy estate? But it was true. Why else would the notion of it turn his stomach into knots?

Hugh took up his damp coat and hat and gloves. "Did the duchess say where she was going after leaving you?"

She would have a plan; some next step to get what she wanted—to find out where Thomas had been the night of the murder.

"She seemed concerned about the time," the magistrate said. "Mentioned something about getting home to the duke before he discovered where she'd gone. The imp. Spunk in spades. Reminds me of my Rebecca," he added with a wistful twitch of his mouth.

Sir Gabriel adored his wife, and she was indeed lively. Hugh sighed. He'd not planned to take the horse back to Violet House himself; visiting the same place too many times wasn't wise, especially if any foot patrols were watching the duchess's home.

"Are your men still watching Violet House?" Hugh inquired. The magistrate arched a brow.

"Give me an hour. I'll send word to have the two assigned to Curzon Street pulled and sent to Knightsbridge—where I've just received word you were seen." He rolled his eyes and waved his hand. "Go. But be cautious. I will deny this meeting ever took place if you are caught."

"And risk allowing anyone to know you like me? Never," Hugh said before leaving.

After all, he'd had plenty of practice keeping secrets.

CHAPTER
NINETEEN

Mildew and the stench of sour ale filled the interior of the hired hackney cab Audrey hailed on Bow Street after leaving Sir Gabriel Poston's office. Upon arriving at the offices, she had sent Carrigan back to Hyde Park, insisting that she would make her way home safely after her meeting with the magistrate. She hadn't anticipated departing the offices with her blood pumping, her pulse streaming in impatience and annoyance. She hadn't noticed the smell when she'd climbed in; nothing had mattered in that moment but leaving Bow Street and the intractable magistrate before she said something she regretted.

The man hadn't taken her seriously. Why had she imagined he would? Just because Hugh and Philip considered her intelligent enough to listen to did not mean any other man would feel the same. She'd been spoiled by the duke and Hugh, and one frustrating conversation with Bow Street's chief magistrate had put her firmly back in her place; a place reserved for silly, hysterical, and overly imaginative ladies. Infuriating! She shifted on the worn bench seat, the stuffed cushion lumpy and hard.

At least Sir Gabriel had not been chomping at the bit to find and arrest Hugh. If anything, he'd seemed worried about his principal officer. He had closed the office door and lowered his baritone voice so as to avoid being overheard—at least that was her suspicion. He'd looked relieved to hear that Hugh was working to find the true murderer and intrigued by the story of April Barlow and the possible Gretna Green elopement. But nothing she'd had to say about Colonel Trenton had affected the magistrate's opinion, which was that the man had no motive—unless Hugh could prove Eloisa's intent had been to expose herself, Bartholomew, and Thomas as illegitimate.

If only she had not tossed aside that gold leaf charm! She was certain the colonel's had been missing from his sidearm when she'd seen him at Hyde Park. Why else would he cover up the tassel with his hand and then so urgently leave the pavilion? Briefly, she'd considered giving the driver instructions to take her to Hyde Park so she could seek him out. But to what end? She couldn't question him in the middle of a military review. It would be beyond the pale.

So instead, she'd instructed the driver to go to Curzon Street. Perhaps Hugh would return with the borrowed mount, or more likely he'd send Sir on the task. It was incredibly frustrating to be cut off from Hugh, to not be able to speak to him. Shivers and jitters attacked her limbs whenever she thought about the possible changing circumstances of Hugh's birth. But it was too cumbersome a notion to even contemplate right then. Whatever the outcome may be, the vital thing was clearing his name.

The hired hack slowed, and gratitude for arriving home nearly made her lightheaded. Or perhaps it was the odor of the cab making her feel that way. Though it was sleeting rain, she breathed in the fresh air as she stepped down onto the drive outside Violet House. It was just in time, too, for she saw Lord

Thornton taking up the reins of his covered curricle, parked just in front of the hackney.

"Your Grace!" He dropped the ribbons and hopped from the conveyance. "I was just about to try Hyde Park. I wondered if you might be at the review."

The front door opened, and a footman sprang forward to pay the hired driver while Audrey invited the physician inside, out of the weather.

"You spoke to the Marcets?" she asked as Barton helped her from her pelisse. Lord Thornton nodded but remained close-lipped until they were able to speak privately in the drawing room. Clearly, he had learned something of interest. Audrey brimmed with agitated hope as the maid bobbed a curtsey and left to fetch tea.

"The Marcets explained the smoke bomb," he said straightaway. "Potassium nitrate, sugar, sodium bicarbonate, and black powder, packed into a hollow tube and activated by a fuse. But that isn't what I found most illuminating."

"What did you, then?"

"The reason for the demonstration in the first place," he replied, a sly grin bowing his lips. Audrey sat and invited him to do the same. "As soon as Mrs. Marcet began to explain, I remembered something from the lecture that I'd forgotten, what with all the commotion after the smoke began filling the hall. The upcoming military review—the mock battles employ scores of smoke bombs to give a realistic effect. The Marcets were engaging the audience on how such a device works and the simple chemistry behind them."

The military review. Audrey sat straighter, her lips parting. "Of course," she whispered. "He would have had ready access to them."

Lord Thornton's handsome face clouded with mystification. "He?"

"Colonel Trenton," she said, and then quickly conveyed what she had to Sir Gabriel, about the sidearm leaf charm, as well as Colonel Trenton's appearance the morning at Lady Reed's.

"They have been training for this review for at least a month," she went on. "Colonel Trenton could have easily been able to procure one of these smoke devices, don't you think?"

"Surely. And the state of his swollen eyes and hoarse throat the following day would indicate he exposed himself to the caustic smoke," Lord Thornton added.

"Colonel Trenton was on the guest list for the soiree that night, but he didn't attend," Audrey said, her mind churning with possible explanations. Her racing thoughts came to a standstill. "The veranda door," she whispered. "It was open when we reached it to escape the smoke, and yet there was no one on the veranda just yet. We were the first."

"He entered through the veranda?"

"It would mean he wouldn't be announced, and perhaps he was not wearing his uniform, only his sidearm," she said, but then shook her head. "Why would Eloisa come into the ballroom?"

"To get away from him?" Lord Thornton shrugged one shoulder. "If he found her in another part of the house and she felt in danger, she might have hoped the other guests would provide safety."

"But he had thought to bring the smoke device with him to provide a bit of panic and chaos, like what occurred at the lecture?" She frowned and felt ill that he had *planned* all this.

After a moment, Lord Thornton spoke again. "Hugh mentioned Joanna Neatham worried Barty wasn't the true heir. I don't know how that could be possible, but surely Trenton would not want Eloisa spreading such information."

Audrey paused before she could say anything about the

truth of Hugh's birthdate; that he'd been born before Bartholomew. Her theory that Fitzgerald and April had eloped was only theory after all, and she did not want to gossip without evidence. Not even to Hugh's closest friend.

Lord Thornton didn't seem to realize she had bit her tongue. He sat forward, elbows upon his thighs, and rubbed his hands together, as if in thought. "It's curious. Hugh never speaks of Trenton. I'm afraid I don't know much about the man."

Audrey hadn't given it much thought, but he was correct. Hugh didn't speak of Colonel Trenton—or Thomas, as he knew him—to her either.

"He despises Barty," he went on.

Audrey met his eye and grinned. "Yes. Quite loquaciously."

Lord Thornton laughed. "He makes no excuses there. But it's almost as if Trenton doesn't exist for Hugh."

The maid arrived with the tea tray then. After their cups were poured and the maid left, Audrey theorized, "Perhaps he has a soft spot for him?"

Lord Thornton shook his head curtly. "No. I've witnessed Hugh and his soft spots. Take Sir and Basil, for example. He grumbles and complains about the pair of them to no end. For Hugh, that is the sign of true fondness."

He sipped his tea while Audrey recalled Hugh's grumbling and complaining *about her*. Perhaps it wasn't the same thing if it was done to her face, but she knew him well enough by now to know he did have a partiality to her. Recalling the few kisses they had shared, she suspected it was more than that.

She was happy when Lord Thornton continued. "No, any mention of Trenton and Hugh is more likely to look like he's swallowed a slimy eel."

At that image, Audrey lowered her tea. Her guest cleared his throat. "My apologies. It's been a long while since I've taken tea in Mayfair. No more talk of eels."

She shook her head and set her saucer and cup on the table. "No, it's not that. It's his reaction. The mention of Colonel Trenton seemed to almost *sicken* him?"

"Yes, I suppose that is it. I've always shrugged it off as his distaste for his half-siblings. But perhaps there is more to the story when it comes to Trenton."

However, after a few moments of quiet, it was clear that conjecture was the only thing they had left to work with. Gossip mongering was the last thing Audrey wanted to partake in, and it seemed the same for Lord Thornton. He thanked her for the tea, and she thanked him for the proof that Colonel Trenton would at least have been knowledgeable on smoke bombs.

He took his leave, going out into the worsening rain. Night would soon be falling too, and all Audrey could think about was where Hugh might be. She hoped he would stay in Wanstead for the night. Out of this rain and in relative safety. Worry for him nibbled away at her as Greer helped her change into a dinner gown. They were having dinner at home that evening, and Audrey knew she ought to use the time alone with Philip to tell him everything having to do with Hugh and the case. She could hardly believe that Philip still did not know of her outing to Mr. Potridge's offices, or anything that had occurred afterward. She had been almost certain the solicitor would have sent word of the duchess's unexpected and unconventional visit.

"You look lovely, Your Grace," Greer pronounced as she finished with the small buttons up the back of the dinner gown —a wine red satin silk, the bodice sewn with onyx beadwork.

"Greer," she began, her mind still turning over what Lord Thornton had said as she stood before the boudoir's oval mirror, "you were in service when the scandal between Lord Neatham and Mr. Marsden took place, weren't you?"

"Yes, Your Grace," she said, fiddling with the short train of the gown, attending to her just as assiduously as she would have had Audrey been about to be presented at a ball.

"Do you recall anything about that time in regard to Colonel Trenton, Lord Neatham's younger brother?"

"How do you mean?" her maid asked, finally stopping to peer at Audrey in the mirror's reflection.

"I'm not sure," she said, realizing how scattered and capricious she must sound. "I suppose I just wondered if you knew anything of the colonel's reputation. His manner."

Greer frowned, faint lines bracketing her lips. She was slight and young in appearance, but in truth Greer must have been in her early thirties. A spinster by any other name, but proud of her position as lady's maid to a duchess. Greer was not an overly warm person; no servant should be, or at least that is what Audrey's mother had always said. But then again, it could be said that Audrey was not a warm person either. She was distant, aloof. Some had even accused her of being a snob. It was a duchess's right, after all. But Audrey was simply guarded. She had learned long ago to only give of herself to those whom she could trust. And she'd found trusting so very challenging.

It was then she realized she had requested her loyal servant to gossip about a peer. And this from Greer, who never spoke a disparaging word against anyone. Audrey's cheeks colored. "I should not have asked. Never mind."

Greer shook her head. "I don't know anything of his manner, I'm afraid. But there was talk," she said, raising a brow. "The servants at Neatham House never believed the accusations against Mr. Marsden. They always suspected another man played the role in Lady Eloisa's ruin."

"And Mr. Marsden was the scapegoat," she replied. Greer parted her lips to speak when a light rap sounded on the door connecting Philip's sitting room to the boudoir.

"Come in," Audrey called.

The duke entered the boudoir, as he often did when crossing between rooms. He was still dressed in what he'd worn to the military review, though his valet had tossed on a sable robe, to warm him, surely.

"You're back," Audrey observed, albeit mundanely. Of course, he was. He was standing right here, wasn't he? Her questions about the colonel had discomfited her. He had something to do with all of this, and the feeling that she was closing in on some dangerous truth had set her nerves aflame.

She wanted to be able to speak to Hugh, to discuss it with him.

But she instead grinned at her husband and dismissed Greer with a nod.

"You look to be feeling better," Philip said, and for a moment Audrey puzzled at the comment. Then, she recalled her excuse for leaving Hyde Park earlier. Cassie and Genie would have informed Philip once they saw him again.

She swallowed. It was time to tell him. "I am. I—"

"Audrey we must discuss something," he said, his words rushed and solemn. Something weighed on his mind; she could always tell when he had disagreeable news to share. It became difficult for him to meet her eyes, and he would prevaricate by inspecting objects close by. Now, it was a gray velvet tufted stool. He ran his hand over the embroidery.

Her head swam as she wondered what could be so serious. Had he heard something about Hugh? Had something happened? Audrey stood with her hands clasped before her, fingers strangling one another.

"Say what you must," she urged after a few protracted moments.

"This isn't easy for me," he said, still fiddling with the velvet tufts. Then he pocketed his hands and turned to face her. "I am leaving for the Continent."

The boudoir swallowed the words, stealing them away before they could properly settle into her mind. Audrey peered at him, bewildered.

"You... The Continent?" she spluttered. "Leaving?"

"Yes." He took a breath, deep enough to expand his chest. His brow furrowed. Pain. She saw it etched there in the lines of his forehead. Not physical pain, but something more profound.

"I have been given a second chance. With Freddie," he said, the last whispered as though his boldness was wavering. But as shock wove its way through Audrey's limbs, Philip held his chin high. "I never stopped loving him, and now that he is here, now that he, too, has been given a second chance, I... I must go."

For how long she gaped at him, she didn't know. But when Philip took her arms and asked her to breathe, to say something, Audrey snapped free of her stupor.

"You cannot be serious."

He released her arms. "I am, very much so. I am in poor health; everyone is aware of that. It isn't so uncommon for the afflicted to travel to warmer climes. The Mediterranean, for instance."

"And you will travel with Mr. Walker?"

"No, that would be...ill advised. We will meet there," he replied.

The velvet tufted stool suddenly appealed to her aspic-like legs. She went to it and sat. "How long will you be away?"

The question was inane. She knew the answer, even if she didn't want to accept it. Could not accept it. The pain she'd seen on his expression deepened. It was pain not for him, but for her.

"I am not returning."

The small dressing room warmed. Then almost instantly, chilled.

"You cannot abandon me," she whispered, her mind reeling.

This wasn't her husband. This wasn't the Duke of Fournier speaking. This man was a stranger inhabiting his body.

"I love you, Audrey; you are my dearest friend. I cannot abide the idea of hurting you, but you must see the truth of the situation—"

"The truth? The truth is that after less than one week of Mr. Walker being back in your life, you've decided to run away together!"

"*The truth* is that neither you nor I have even the slimmest chance at happiness if I stay," he said, his voice rising with conviction.

She glared at him, refusing to permit he was even fractionally correct. She was far too furious for that. "So, you will tarnish the Fournier name and legacy, you will abandon your duty to it, to your estates and those who depend upon you, while you live out your life in *warmer climes*?"

Her temper was quickly overtaking her, causing her to raise her voice. She slammed her jaw shut and clenched her teeth. Risking any of the servants overhearing would be a disaster. Even Greer.

"No, I do not plan to ruin the Fournier name by living in open scandal on the Continent," he replied tightly, then lowered his voice. "I plan to die."

Audrey balked. Her festering rage dropped to a simmer. "I don't understand. Are you..." She slid from the stool, but her legs wouldn't hold her, so she sat down again. "Are you so very ill?"

A flicker of a smile touched his mouth and then was gone. "No. I'm not as ill as that."

Understanding whipped her, sparking lash after sparking lash. "You are going to fake your own death?"

"It is the only way, don't you see? For both of us. I would

never leave you to shoulder the burden or embarrassment of my choice."

"But Michael, Cassie, Tobias...they will be destroyed. They love you. You are their brother. You would let them believe you are dead when you're not?"

Guilt cut across his face. It was genuine, Audrey knew, but she also suspected that it would not be enough to stop him.

"I have given this thought, Audrey. More than you know. And not just now, because of Freddie. The plan has crossed my mind before." He sighed and came toward her, though he stopped short of reaching for her hands, which were balled into fists in the lap of her dinner gown. Her throat thickened. Betrayal poured into her like molten lead. He had thought of leaving her before?

"Michael has Genie, and now, a son. He will fill his home with children and love. And anyhow, Michael will be a much better duke than I ever could be. You know it to be true."

The title would pass to Michael, then to little George. She refused to agree verbally, stubbornness stitching her lips together. But Philip was correct. He had always been more academic and closed off, while Michael was business minded and outgoing, social and commanding. Philip had always given the impression that he was a reluctant duke, lamenting that he had been firstborn. To him, the title was a baleful duty, not a privilege.

"Tobias will leave university and make his way in the world. He has friends and," Philip shrugged, "he has always been much closer to Michael anyhow. Cassie will soon marry, and her life will be full and busy. They will all recover."

"And what of me? I love you too. You are telling me you will never come back, that I will never see you again."

"You love me as a friend," he reminded her, chucking her on the chin. He probably meant it to be affectionate, but she found it patronizing. Audrey forced her knees to lock as she stood and skirted around him, needing the open air of her bedroom.

She stalked toward the window and opened the sash an inch. It helped to clear her head. "So, I am to be a widow." She then huffed mirthlessly. "A counterfeit widow."

"No one will be wise to it. And as a widow, you can remarry, this time for legitimate reasons."

"There will be nothing legitimate about it!" Audrey whirled to face him. Saw the remorse in his eyes. "Any marriage will be illegal. Any future children will be illegitimate."

How could Philip honestly believe this to be to her benefit? Her heart might long for Hugh, but she could never lie to him. And once he knew Philip was alive and well somewhere in the Mediterranean, he would never agree to the risk, not after spending his whole life as by-blow. How could she bring any child into the world knowing that they would be born on the other side of the blanket? The child's future would be in constant jeopardy. Audrey was not a mother, but she felt a sudden, fierce pang of obligation. Of compulsion. To protect them from any disgrace.

"They would never be that," Philip said, an edge of impatience limning his words. This conversation was not progressing as he thought it might, apparently. Audrey reveled in that, at least. She didn't want to make any of this easy for him. "Even if I were to be discovered—which I won't be—whatever children you bear would be mine."

"What good would that do? You would be a criminal for falsifying your death. We would all be tainted by scandal."

Philip, lost for words perhaps, threw up his hands and walked away, toward the door. She wanted him to leave, to give her room to breathe and think. Far too many thoughts cluttered her mind, though not just concerning Philip's plot. The question of scandal for any future children drew parallels to what Lord and Lady Neatham would go through, should it come to light that Hugh was the true heir. Their young children, while legitimate, would be ruined. Their secure futures, ripped away from them. Surely, the viscountess would feel the same motherly pang of obligation, that same compulsion to protect her children.

What would a mother not do to safeguard her children from such devastation?

"Audrey?" Philip's voice came to her as if muffled. "Are you listening to me?"

She realized she was staring at the carpet. Her eyes snapped up to meet his. "The viscountess."

He knit his brow. "What?"

Audrey paced forward, her mind spinning. Lady Reed. She had been privy to the Joanna Neatham's worry that Barty was illegitimate...and she was also the current viscountess's great aunt.

The connection pulled taut in Audrey's mind, like a slack string suddenly yanked tight. Even though she knew not what it meant, she trusted it.

"I'm sorry, I must get some air," she said breathlessly to Philip. Without waiting for him to respond, she rushed to her boudoir, tore down her cloak from the wardrobe, and then hurried from the bedroom.

Her feet moved as if of their own accord. Where she was going, she wasn't certain, but she knew she had to follow that taut string. It brought her to the kitchens and to the sudden knowledge that she had to summon Carrigan.

To her surprise, and perhaps serendipity, she came to a halt when she saw Sir lounging at the servant's long table, a plate of food before him. Mrs. Comstock jumped to and bobbed her head toward Audrey.

"Your Grace, may I help you? Is there something you needed?"

Greer, who'd been seated across from Sir, stood quickly with a look of alarm and contrition. Sir, meanwhile, finished his forkful of mash.

"I need to speak to the boy," Audrey said, causing almost the entire kitchen staff to come to a halt. They were in the middle of preparing dinner for her and the duke, and her appearance was more than irregular.

"Young man," the cook hissed at Sir, who was quickly spearing his long beans and shoving them into his mouth. "The duchess is speaking to you. Get up. My apologies, Your Grace, the lad is an errand boy of sorts, and it seems he is in wont of manners."

Sir scrubbed his nose and stood. "What can I do for you, duchess?"

Audrey started for the back door, and being wise, Sir followed. Once they stood upon the backstep, alone, she spoke. "Is Mr. Marsden back in London yet?"

The boy lifted a bony shoulder. "Don't know. Why?"

"I need to speak to Lady Neatham. Her children..." She gulped a calming breath as heart began to pound. "I might have thought of something."

"I'll come with you," the boy said.

"That's not necessary."

"Mister Hugh told me to keep my blinkers on you," Sir said.

"I'll have Carrigan," she said, warming at the idea of Hugh posting his trusted associate at Violet House to keep watch over her. "It's more important for you to stay here and tell Mr. Marsden where I've gone, if he arrives."

"He won't return the horse himself," Sir said as Audrey started for the mews lane and the stables.

"I'm sorry, I must go," she called back. She didn't care in the least about the horse. Though she didn't yet know what she would say to Lady Neatham, Audrey couldn't stay in her room, drowning in Philip's revelation and in her questions about the viscountess. She would just have to devise a plan on the way to Neatham House.

Nنone of the conveyances parked along Kensington Square near Neatham House resembled any belonging to the Duchess of Fournier. Hugh looked for Carrigan and his broad shoulders in the various driver's boxes but couldn't see him either.

He'd allowed Sir Gabriel the hour he'd requested to clear out the two Bow Street constables who'd been assigned to Curzon Street. The night before, he'd arrived within the duchess's carriage, but they would have certainly seen him tonight, riding in on the borrowed mount. However, before Hugh had even reached the mews behind Violet House, he'd met with Sir. The boy had been keeping his own watch.

The duchess had left Violet House abruptly, Sir reported. She'd been gabbing on about Lady Neatham and her children and how she thought she'd figured something out. With a stroke of alarm, Hugh had kept Fournier's horse and ridden it to Neatham House as quickly as possible. Sir, meanwhile, was to go to St James's Square and fetch Thornton.

Audrey should have arrived at Kensington Square by now.

Hugh embraced the falling darkness as he dismounted and looped the reins over a post, his gaze hinged on the lit windows of Neatham House. Given the time—just before six o'clock—Barty and his wife should be at home. It was too early to be out for the evening, and it was unfashionable to still be out making calls or turning through Hyde Park.

Perhaps Carrigan had parked further around the square, away from Barty's residence. Looking upon it now gave Hugh the same adverse swirl, low in his gut, that the place always inspired. Neatham House wasn't a home of fond memories. Hugh had always preferred the viscount's Surrey estate, near Cranleigh. There, at least, he could go off into the fields and woods; he could keep the company of the servants and stable hands more easily too. Here, in London, Neatham House had felt like a prison.

One that might have swallowed up Audrey.

Again, he wondered what she could have possibly been thinking coming here, seeking out Lady Neatham. What about her children had she discovered? He stood there, next to his horse, stymied. He couldn't very well go knocking on the front door again.

"Don't move," a gruff voice said from behind Hugh. At the same time, something hard pressed between his ribs. He knew the shape.

"Not the finest evening for a stroll around Kensington Square, is it?" the man said with a harsh laugh. "Keep your hands on the reins of your horse, still-like."

"Who are you?" Hugh asked, but a waft of the man hit his nostrils, and Hugh knew. Horse and urine. Rasping voice. This was the man who took the folio from Audrey.

Answers stacked up, one after the other. Why Audrey had set out for Neatham House, why she'd mentioned the viscountess and her children. Why this man would have wanted the folio.

"You're working for Lady Neatham," Hugh said, gripping the leather reins, as instructed. The horse shifted uneasily, sensing his tension and the looming danger.

"She thought you might figure out what's what after I swiped those papers. Said you'd probably come around the square, though I didn't think you'd be that stupid."

"I do love to surprise," Hugh said. "Well? Aren't you going to take me to her?"

The man guffawed. "Into the house? 'Course not. I'm to dispose of you in private," he explained, saying this last with an air of reverence, as if it was some great honor he'd been tasked with.

In private? Hugh gathered that no one else in Neatham House knew about this man. Lila, the viscountess, had hired him on her own, acting in secret. Without her husband's knowledge.

Which meant Hugh had an opportunity. He had leverage over the viscountess.

"No, I suppose she wouldn't want you stinking up her fine rooms," Hugh said, and as the man started to grate out another rasp of laughter, he twisted to the side and spun, knocking the man's arm out to the side. He landed a facer and heard the crack of the man's nose. The man stumbled, and Hugh threw his weight, taking him firmly to the ground. Two bashes of his wrist against the hard cobbles, and the pistol clattered free. Hugh leaped to his feet and kicked the weapon, sending it skidding off into the darkness.

"Now," Hugh panted, "perhaps we'll go see the viscountess together."

The man rolled to his knees to try and stand, but Hugh caught him around the neck and dragged him to his feet. This sod wasn't so different from the many criminals he'd arrested before, and as he towed him straight to Neatham House's front door, then kicked the painted wood by way of knocking, Hugh almost felt a burst of nostalgia for his foot patrol days. The man squirmed and swore, but Hugh had him locked under the chin, applying just enough pressure to cut off some of his air flow and make him compliant.

The front door began to open slowly, but just one glimpse at Hugh and the man tussling on the front step, and the footman made to shut the door and lock it again. Hugh gave it a helpful shove with his foot, knocking the footman back into a table and sending him to the floor.

Hugh dragged the footpad toward the stairs, directly ahead. The man's feet stumbled and slipped, but Hugh wrenched onward, his destination the first level, where the private rooms of the viscount and viscountess were located.

Several voices shouted from below, followed by pounding feet.

He couldn't move fast enough, not with the hired man weighing him down. With seconds to spare before a pair of footmen could lunge at him from behind, Hugh reached the landing and tossed the man to the pale green carpet, creating an obstacle for the servants, who stopped short before they might trip over the man.

"What the devil is going on here!" Barty shouted as he entered the landing. He spotted Hugh, and at the same moment, Hugh made out the weapon held in his brother's hand. It was a muff pistol; he'd likely grabbed for it at the resounding commotion in the front hall.

"You!" He aimed the pistol at him. "Parker, summon the police! You are going to swing from a rope on Tower Hill, Marsden."

One of the footmen descended the stairs, presumably to flag down the closest foot patrol.

Hugh heaved for breath and gestured to the man who'd finally staggered to his feet. Blood streamed from his nose, and he'd lost his hat. "This man attacked the Duchess of Fournier in her home; she will attest to this. I am placing him under arrest for that crime—and for the murders of Eloisa and Lady Reed."

The desired effect came through.

"I didn't kill no one!" the man barked.

With golden timing, Lady Neatham exited a room, onto the narrow first level landing. Her wide eyes jumped from Hugh to the man she'd hired, then to her husband. She made to retreat into her room.

"Going so soon, my lady?" Hugh called. "Please, stay. This is your handiwork, after all."

She hitched her chin, her fists curled into the skirts of her dress. "I don't take your meaning. Barty, what is happening here?"

"Lila's handiwork? My god, Marsden, what madness consumes you? My dear, leave us."

Barty's useless arm was tucked up into a sling, resting upon his paunch. His wife's stare lingered on the hired man a moment too long as she hesitated in the doorway to her room.

"You're wondering if you paid him well enough to keep his mouth shut," Hugh said to her, ignoring his half-brother and the pistol. Muff pistols were known for their inaccuracy; one needed to practically press the barrel to its target if they wanted to hit their mark.

"Don't be absurd," she hissed. "Whatever could I want with the likes of him?"

She glared at the crass footpad in revulsion. What *would* the viscountess want with him?

"Of course," Hugh said as what Sir mentioned the previous

day, about another solicitor's office being turned over, came clear. "It was Tipper and Sons. That's the office you had this footpad turn over, not realizing that the solicitor your husband employs is not the same as our father's solicitor, Mr. Potridge. You were searching for the documents in the wrong place."

More servants crowded up on the stairs to see what the commotion was, but none of them grabbed for Hugh. With Barty's pistol aimed at him, no one wished to be in the potential line of fire. He scowled at Hugh. Then his wife. "What documents? Lila, what is he on about?"

"Don't listen to him," she said sharply. "He is insane. He killed Eloisa."

"How did you know she was in London?" Hugh asked her, his heavy breaths evening out, his heartrate dropping. He needed to think clearly if he wanted to get out of this without irons first being clapped onto his wrists.

The viscountess sneered but didn't answer.

"Lady Reed is your aunt," Hugh went on, piecing it together. Realizing what Audrey must have grasped. "She warned you, didn't she? Told you what the late viscountess confessed to her on her deathbed."

Lila Neatham's coloring drained.

"What is all this claptrap?" Barty asked, his attention darting frantically between his wife and Hugh.

The hired man used the distraction to break for the stairs. He pushed a footman aside and then a maid as he fled, leaping three or four steps at a time. Hugh watched him go, unconcerned.

"Where is that man going?" Barty demanded. "Who in the blazes is he anyhow?"

Hugh warmed to the opening. "He's the man your wife hired to kill Eloisa."

She gargled on air and a half scream. "No! I did no such thing! I gave him no orders for that."

"You cur!" Barty re-leveled the pistol at him, after having let it slip as he became addled.

"But you did give him orders to turn over the wrong solicitor's offices, and then, when you realized your mistake, homed in on Potridge's offices. But the duchess got there first, so your man attacked her and took the documents regarding April Barlow." The duchess. Hugh's focus diverted. "Where is she? The Duchess of Fournier was to call on you."

Lady Neatham scowled. "I have not seen her."

"Enough about the duchess. Tell me who this April Barlow chit is and what documents you refer to," Barty commanded.

Time was running thin. Kensington Square wasn't far from Hyde Park, and there would be a number of foot patrolmen covering the area. It wouldn't take long for the dispatched footman to find one and bring him back. Hugh didn't have long. He needed to be blunt.

"April Barlow is our father's first wife," Hugh said, expelling the truth like gaseous air that had been trapped in his lungs. "She is my mother."

Disbelief surged across the viscount's face, quickly followed by understanding. Barty was a lot of things, but never a simpleton. He could calculate and connive with the best of them. Though, perhaps not so thoroughly as his wife.

"Impossible," he breathed. "You're a bastard. Nanny Catherine was your mother."

Hugh could sympathize with the denial. He had felt an abundance of it himself.

"Nanny Catherine was hired to be my mother. I was given to her when I was six months of age, when Miss Barlow gave me up. She left me, the same way she left our father. They had eloped—"

"Leave," the viscountess said, though she wasn't speaking to Hugh. She looked past him, to the servants crowding the top of the stairs and the landing behind him. "All of you, go! Leave us."

The footmen and maids did as they were bid when the viscount did not refute his wife's command, though surely the butler would stand his post at the bottom of the stairs, awaiting the arrival of the police.

"Shoot him, Bartholomew," the viscountess said once they were alone, her voice shaking. "He's lying. He's dangerous!"

"In many ways, I am. I could take everything from you," Hugh said. "But I'm not lying. And I'm not a killer. Barty, call off the police. I didn't kill Eloisa. Let's talk this through."

"There is nothing to talk through!" Lady Neatham's eyes gleamed with frustrated tears "Do you know what this means, Bartholomew? You are *illegitimate*. You, Eloisa, Thomas, all of you!"

"*Lila*." Barty sounded peculiarly calm, and his grip on the pistol was firm again. He stared balefully at Hugh. "Was there an annulment?"

With a shake of his head, Barty's eyes dulled another degree.

Lady Neatham rushed to her husband's side, suddenly pleading with him. "Aunt Mary told me there was no proof, that your mother could never find it, but then the documents Mr. Felix brought me, they stated this horrible man's birth date," she said, gesticulating toward Hugh, "and the agreements between your father and Miss Barlow and Catherine Marsden. But I've burned them." She clutched at his useless arm, tucked in the sling. "No one ever need know. Think of our children. Think of their futures! Shoot him!"

Barty's face, his body, had become a block of wood.

"Lady Neatham, you are backed into a corner," Hugh said.

"Bow Street's chief magistrate already knows everything. He is fetching the certificate of marriage as we speak. Proof of the late viscount's first marriage will soon be in hand, if it is not already."

"So you can take my title," Barty said softly.

"To hell with your title!" Hugh rasped. "This is about Eloisa. She wanted April Barlow found, she wanted the truth exposed so you would be ruined. The truth is motive for someone who would benefit from silencing her."

He held the viscountess's glare. Panic and fear had narrowed her pupils to pinpricks. She gaped as his implication settled.

"I didn't kill her! I've already told you. I had no idea she was even in London until *you* stormed in here, shouting to Bartholomew about it." She looked between Hugh and Barty, seeking their belief. "It is true! When you mentioned April Barlow, I knew my aunt's warning had merit. I had to find and destroy any evidence there might be, but I would never have harmed Eloisa. I didn't even hire Mr. Felix until the following day!"

She wasn't lying. The beseeching expression, the rattled pleading...Hugh had born witness to many pleas like it before. The guilty made excuses for their behavior. The innocent pleaded with those around them to believe them.

That meant Mr. Felix couldn't have been the man who had visited April Barlow at the Field Street finishing school, days before the murder. He hadn't been the one to threaten to send both "Susan Smith" and the headmistress to the bottom of the Thames. That man had not so much as mentioned the secret marriage. Because he had not known to. He'd been there to simply keep Eloisa and her child out of London. A child Barty knew had not died.

And if Barty knew, so did Thomas.

Hugh had thought Eloisa's nervousness the day she'd visited his home on Bedford Street was due to Barty discovering she was in town. But what if it had not been her elder brother she was hiding from?

The crackling storm of disgust and hatred roiled in Hugh's stomach anew as he met Barty's level stare.

"Where is Thomas?" Hugh's voice didn't sound like his own, but like it had clawed its way up from under the heavy rubble of buried secrets. Gasping for air. For answers.

A pea whistle in the distance reached them on the landing, and the muzzle of the muff pistol drifted to the side as Barty's expression softened. Then, it snapped back into alignment with Hugh's chest. "I can't let you."

"You know it was him," Hugh said as more whistles sounded. "You knew back then too. You knew what he'd done. And you turned it on me then, just as you've done now."

Barty shook his head. "I have to protect my family."

An amalgamation of pity and hatred nearly consumed Hugh as the full truth came clear.

"Bartholomew," the viscountess said, clutching at him again. "Do it. You are within your rights. He broke in here, tried to attack us."

He'd stood in Barty's line of fire before, the last time he'd lied to cover up Thomas's offenses. He would have gladly killed Hugh to conceal his brother's warped conduct. Now, Hugh waited for the flash of gunpowder, the report of the pistol.

But the viscount lowered his arm, and Hugh understood. He turned and ran from the landing. The servant's stairwell wasn't far, and he could take it to the side entrance to the house. Behind him, the viscountess screamed. His hand was on the knob to the servant's stairwell when a vase on a pedestal table just behind him exploded into shards.

He took the steps like a storm wind, sailing down without

drawing breath, grateful the layout of the house was still engrained in his mind. Only a few maids screeched and jumped aside as he ran to the servant's entrance and burst outside, into the mews. He ran toward the head of the mews. A clamor was building out front of Neatham House, and as he reached the side street that fed into square, Hugh paused. There was nothing for it—he'd have to leave Fournier's horse behind.

A curricle clattered past the head of the mews and Hugh pulled back, into the shadows. But not fast enough. The driver whistled to the horses and brought them to shuddering halt.

"Mister Hugh!" Sir's rasping whisper came from the stopped curricle.

"Goddamn it, Marsden, get in the bloody rig!" *Thornton*.

Hugh scurried over and hauled himself up, Thornton slapping the reins and tossing him practically into Sir's lap.

"What in Hades possessed you to go to Neatham House again, you idiot?" Thornton said as he made a tight turn to avoid the square.

Hugh grabbed Sir's coat collar. "You said the duchess came here."

"She did!" The boy peeled Hugh's fingers from his collar. "Said she was having Carrigan bring her."

"I think we were spotted." Thornton twisted around to peer behind them. Sure enough, pea whistles choruses behind them in the vicinity of the square.

"Well then, drive faster," Sir said.

"The park." Hugh pointed toward the gate into Hyde Park. "We'll lose them in there."

It was dark now, and the moon not yet risen fully. Gas lamps lit some of the paths and lanes near the edges of the park, but nothing of the interior. One could get lost in there at night.

Hugh stilled, the clatter of Thornton's rig dissolving behind a thought. Clear across the park, was Mayfair and the Curzon Gate. It was entirely likely Carrigan had come through the park, on his way to Kensington Square.

"Turn off the King's Road at your first chance," Hugh said.

"Yes, there are too many lamps," Thornton agreed.

"That's not the only reason," Hugh said, intuition prickling his skin. "She is here, in the park. Something is wrong."

TWENTY-ONE

A mounting sense of futility accompanied the fading evening light. Audrey sat perched on the edge of the bench seat, her nose practically to the glass of the window and her eyes straining to see more than a few yards off the gravel path into Hyde Park.

Carrigan had spent the last hour directing the horses around the circumference of the park, along bisecting footpaths, across the Serpentine Bridge, up and down Rotten Row and the Ladies' Mile. He'd even gone up to the Cumberland Gate at the corner of Oxford Street, where Lady Neatham would surely have no desire to walk. Some four hundred acres in total, the park began to empty as Audrey instructed Carrigan to make another turn near the wide western edge of the Serpentine.

In her heart, she knew what she was doing: avoiding her necessary visit to Neatham House. It was no longer a fashionable hour to amble through the park, and the military review had come to a close. The red uniformed foot soldiers and horse guards had returned to their barracks, leaving the plains of the park an ugly sea of churned up mud, snow, and grass. Philip always lamented these reviews and the state in which they left the ground here.

Philip. No, she could not think of him or his confounding plan to abscond to the Continent with Freddie Walker. There would be time for that later, though she didn't look forward to it then, either. But for right now, Hugh's predicament was unfolding, and Lady Neatham may have played a role.

Her aunt, Lady Reed, had heard the previous viscountess's feverish deathbed confession, and it was possible that she would have warned her niece against marrying a man who might be illegitimate. It could have planted a seed of knowledge within Lila Neatham's mind, which might have produced a bounty of fear. For her children, for herself. Audrey felt something slightly similar when thinking of the risk Philip would stack against her by leaving, by falsifying his death. She would have much to lose, should his actions be discovered.

But perhaps it wouldn't come to that. He might see how flagrant and perilous such a deception was, and wind up doing the responsible, sensible, thing.

As the carriage had rattled around the park in seemingly endless circles, Audrey tried to contrive what she would say to Lady Neatham, should she spy her walking with her maid or a few companions. Worse still, what would she say to her now that she had no other avenue but to go to Kensington Square? The words eluded her. Which made her feel stupid and powerless.

Just as she'd felt when Philip had announced he was leaving her.

Audrey rubbed the sudden sting at the tip of her nose and blinked back tears. *Not now.* They had lost all light and night shadows swarmed the park. About a hundred yards ahead, the wide, mile-long gravel path of Rotten Row, the entirety of it lit by oil lamps, shone like a beacon.

"To Neatham House," she called, raising her voice so Carrigan could hear.

He nickered to the horses, and they answered with renewed vigor. It only lasted a few moments. A male voice hollered loudly, hailing Carrigan.

"Hallo there! Might I ask your assistance?" the deep voice called.

Audrey's carriage slowed. The man went on to complain about the muddy ruts in the ground from the review, and how his buggy's wheel had sunk into it. Might Carrigan assist in pulling it free?

The carriage rocked as her driver descended. The top of his hat appeared in the window. "I'll be but a moment, Your Grace, if you'll permit it."

"Of course, Carrigan, go on." What would a few more minutes of evasion cost her?

There was nothing for it. She would simply have to come out and speak plainly to the viscountess. Ask her, directly, what she knew about Miss April Barlow.

She was busy picturing the shocked expression Lady Neatham would surely react with when a grunt and the sounds of a scuffle reached through the lacquered wood of her carriage. Audrey turned her ear and sat still.

"Carrigan?" she said after a prolonged silence. Much too silent. The man and her driver had ceased speaking. Philip had often warned her against entering the park at night, for fear of footpads and thieves, but she'd thought...with Carrigan with her...

Her pulse spiked, and Audrey slid along the bench seat toward the left door. Their muffled voices had been coming from the right. That instinct proved fruitful, for with a sudden jerk, the right-side door flew open. The burning oil lamp set into the quilted carriage wall shed its light over a familiar face. *Colonel Trenton.*

"Your Grace," he drawled with a callous twist of his lips.

She shoved the left door open and gathered up her skirts before leaping to the ground. It was a good three feet, and she landed off center, her slipper skidding to the side in a patch of mud. She hadn't taken the time before leaving Violet House to change into hardier boots. The heels of those, however, would have hindered her, so she was thankful for the flat soles as she dashed away from the stopped carriage, into the darkened lawn of Hyde Park. Still, in her panic, it felt as though she were running through a pool of honey.

Back at the carriage, she heard a renewed scuffle—grunts and groans as Carrigan, no doubt, recovered and threw himself back into the fight with Colonel Trenton. Her mind spun as she realized what was happening. Trenton had attacked her driver. He planned to attack *her*. Because she had been correct: He had killed Eloisa. His sidearm had lost the triple leaf charm in that ballroom, and she had given away her interest at the pavilion. She was a complete fool!

And now, he'd found her alone in Hyde Park.

"Running won't help you, Your Grace!"

The colonel must have broken away from Carrigan. He sounded a short distance behind her, his voice strident, as if he was running too. What had he done to her driver? Worry for Carrigan evaporated with the fear of Colonel Trenton next overtaking her. He was a soldier and could certainly outstrip her in a foot race without effort. Her head start was languishing. She needed to find a place to hide, and quickly.

Twilight had nearly faded to full dark, making visibility poor. It was like trying to see through a pool of spilled ink as her legs carried her straight into it. She knew the footpaths well enough to know that there were shrubs and trees scattered throughout the lawns, and ahead, the shallow Serpentine.

"I never wanted this to happen," Colonel Trenton called. Panic seared like a hot brand into her chest. *He was closer.*

Blast! Hugh had told her to keep a knife or muff pistol on her person, but she had not thought to heed the advice. How she wished she had even a pen knife in her pocket right then.

In the dim moonlight, a gathering of trees ahead took shape. If she could see them, so could her pursuer, and he could surely see her figure as well. But she had no other choice. Audrey plunged between the thick, knobby trunks of two trees. The soggy ground beneath her slurped at her slippers, threatening to tug them clear off. And then, a deep hollow in the lawn swallowed her foot whole. She fell, slamming onto the ground, though she felt no pain—only the terror of knowing the mistake would be fatal.

"Stop," Colonel Trenton commanded as Audrey attempted to get to her feet. She froze, her knees pressing the skirt of her dinner gown into the wet sod, her ruined gloves planted ahead of her.

With her back to him, she had the horrible thought that this was how Eloisa had died, with her back to her enemy. Audrey spun around, falling to the ground on her backside, to at least look her attacker in the eye. He stood no more than three arm lengths away. He'd stopped running and was now huffing for air as he leveled a pistol at her. She noticed that he was no longer in uniform.

"A buggy wheel stuck in the mud, that was your diversion this time? No smoke explosion?" Her voice quavered as a deluge of fury and fear warmed her.

"I wondered at my good fortune when I saw your driver circling the deserted paths."

She gritted her teeth at his cavalier tone and chided herself for not taking Rotten Row straight through the park's Kensington gate. For stonewalling instead of being forthcoming and brave.

The grainy snow and the pooling mud shifted underneath her palms, seeping through the lace. Her fingers curled and felt the hard surface of a rock, submerged in the mud. It wouldn't be much use against a pistol, but it was all she had. She began to pull at it, attempting to dislodge it from the mud without Colonel Trenton noticing.

"You killed your own *sister*," she said, her pulse knocking in her neck, causing her voice to undulate. "To keep her from telling the truth?"

"What do you know of the truth?" He no longer sounded confident, but harsh. *Fearful.*

Audrey watched him, conscious of the fact that he could fire off a shot at any moment. Why had he not yet done so? They were secluded here, without another wandering soul in the whole of four hundred acres, or at least it felt that way.

"You would not be aiming your pistol at me if I didn't know everything."

He growled. "Hugh promised Eloisa he would never tell a soul. Why would he tell you?"

What could he mean by that? Hugh had not mentioned promising Eloisa any such thing. Unless the colonel was speaking of something else, some other secret.

She had nothing to lose. Audrey blushed as she lied through her teeth. "He has told me. We are...quite intimate."

A dry, teasing laugh emitted from his throat. "Ahh, that blackguard, showing his stripes after all. Dallying with a married woman." He took a step forward, and Audrey tried to scuttle back, but her skirts were tangled beneath her. However, her fingers shifted the submerged rock. She kept trying to wriggle it free.

"And tell me, Your Grace," he continued. "Were you repulsed?"

Repulsed? Her clawing fingers stilled. That was an odd word to use to describe their illegitimacy. "No. Of course not."

"You lie," he seethed, his mean humor flipping over toward anger again. "It *is* repulsive. It's revolting, don't you think I know that?" His voice carried. Audrey could only hope someone heard it. But if she screamed for help, he would certainly shoot. Her fingers scrabbled at the edges of the buried rock. It wasn't large, perhaps about the size of her hand.

"No one understood us. But it was love," he said, a small crack in that last uttered word.

What was he saying? Was he speaking of *Eloisa*?

Then, gently, like the barest tug of a thread coming loose on one of her silk stockings, comprehension unraveled through Audrey's mind. A torrent of sickening dread buried her. Her fingers, aching from digging through the cold mud, paused again. Colonel Trenton spoke of love, but not that which existed between brother and sister.

"It wasn't Hugh," she whispered. Of course, she'd known Hugh would never have ruined his half-sister. The notion had been absurd, it had been repellant. She had believed it to be so debased that she'd felt disgust for Bartholomew for even accusing him of it. And yet...

"Hugh discovered you," she speculated and was rewarded.

"El begged him to keep quiet. He promised he would," he said. "But I knew he was lying. He meant to call me out. He meant to kill me."

Shock transformed into denial, and then, with bile curdling in her stomach, certainty arrived.

Hugh had discovered Trenton and Eloisa. Together.

"Bartholomew called him out first," she realized, "before Hugh could issue the challenge to you."

The new viscount had either not believed Hugh's claim...or he had, and the desire to protect his family name and reputation had eclipsed his moral honor. But Hugh lived. And still, he never breathed a word about it. *A promise to Eloisa.*

"You thought she was in London to expose *that* truth," she said. "But how did you know she was even here?"

"Do you think I would not have had someone watching her all these years?" he said, becoming agitated. "I was kept informed, and when I learned she intended to sneak to London and why, I could not allow it. When I found her in London, I warned her off. But she wouldn't listen. She said she no longer cared; that she would see us all ruined. And that Lady Reed knew everything."

Air fled from Audrey's lungs, and she went dizzy, even seated as she was upon the ground. He'd gotten it all wrong. Eloisa wanted to ruin him, yes, but not by exposing *that* secret. And Lady Reed had heard Joanna's death bed confession, not the other secret.

"You knew she planned to go to Lady Reed's soiree," she speculated. "You followed her there. With your upcoming nuptials, you couldn't let either of them expose you."

He said nothing, but she knew it to be true. The bride was wealthy, Lady Reed had imparted, and if Eloisa were to expose what the colonel truly was, he would be shunned. He'd lose everything.

The trembling of a light and the clattering of a conveyance nearby stole her attention. She craned her neck behind her to see it.

"Utter one sound, and I will shoot," Colonel Trenton warned.

He had one shot in that pistol. One chance to hit his mark. He was close enough to his immobile target to manage. But in the pitch dark, his chances of hitting a moving target would drastically reduce. This was her last chance.

Audrey gripped the rock and finally ripped it free from the mud. She hurled it toward his head and heard it connect. Trenton grunted and swore as she rolled to her knees and leaped to her feet. Hiking her skirts, she ran toward the carriage, which seemed to be getting closer.

"Help!" she screamed. "Help!"

"Audrey!"

The answering shout seared through her. *Hugh's voice*. It sounded from her left, and she veered in that direction. A hand wrenched her arm and yanked her back.

"Stop!" The colonel's command rang through Audrey's ear as he pinned her to his side. Her ribs screamed in pain as a hard object pressed against them.

Hugh materialized through the darkness. "Let her go. This has nothing to do with her."

The clatter of the carriage was upon them next, its dual lanterns tossing light across the lawn. It gradually illuminated Hugh, his hat gone, his hands raised as he stepped closer. He held no weapon.

"Stay back," Colonel Trenton ordered, the pistol digging into her ribs harder. She let out an involuntary yelp of pain, and Hugh stopped.

"If you harm her, Thomas, there is nothing in this world that will keep me from killing you."

"Alas, dear brother, you should have thought of the duchess's safety before you dragged her into our family business."

"He told me nothing—*you did*," Audrey said, even though just breathing and expanding of her ribs was excruciating. "Eloisa wasn't going to expose you for what you did to her. She was going to expose another family secret. Your illegitimacy. Yours and hers and Bartholomew's."

His body stiffened. "What?"

"Release the duchess." Lord Thornton's command came from the vicinity of the carriage behind them. "Marsden's hands may be empty, but mine are not."

The physician appeared in Audrey's limited scope of vision. He came to stand a short distance from Hugh, and he held a pistol, the barrel of it aimed at her and Colonel Trenton.

He ignored Lord Thornton and squeezed Audrey tighter within the grip of his bracing arm. "What do you mean, illegitimacy?"

"The circumstances of your birth don't matter. Not now. I will kill you before this night is over, you primordial miscreant," Hugh said, a harsh, mirthless laugh scraping up his throat. "Eloisa came here for revenge, but not the revenge you believed. Did you stop to think what she could possibly gain from telling all of society what you did to her? About who the father of her child really is?"

With a swell of loathing, Audrey tried to peel herself away from the colonel. He wouldn't relent.

"I loved her," he said, his voice so rough she felt the claim reverberate from his chest into her back.

"You were always a coward," Hugh said. "Slinking off into the shadows, letting your brother fight your battles for you. You have no idea how many times I have dreamed of putting a bullet into your warped brain. The only reason I didn't was because Eloisa begged me not to." Hugh held out his arms wide. "Well, she is no longer here, is she? I challenge you to a duel, Thomas. Here. Now. As it should have been six years ago."

Colonel Trenton went stone still. He didn't speak. Didn't even breathe. A coward, Hugh had called him, and Audrey could feel it in those silent moments. His fear, his cowardice.

"Release the duchess," Hugh said. "Thornton, give me your pistol."

The physician closed the space between them, extending his arm to hand over the weapon. Audrey felt the uncoiling of the colonel's muscles, the diminishing pressure of the pistol against her ribs, and she knew what he would do.

"Hugh—!" she screamed a second before she was shoved aside. The hard ground jolted through her shoulder and back as the reports of two pistols, one right after the other, cracked through the air.

Close to her, Colonel Trenton erupted into howls of agony. The pitiful sound burrowed into her ears, and with it came relief. He'd been struck. But what of Hugh? She pushed herself up and was staggering to her feet when a body collided into hers. A pair of arms wrapped around her, practically lifting her off her feet. A hand braced the back of her head and held her close.

"Audrey." Hugh breathed into her hair, loosed from its pins, and hanging around her shoulders. She instantly melted against him. "Are you injured? Did he hurt you?"

Recalling the second shot, she pulled back and looked Hugh over in the dim light of the carriage lanterns. "You weren't hit?"

"Not even a nick," he said, breathing hard. He raked some of her hair away from her face, his expression still somber. "But you are bleeding. Your head—"

"I fell." She must have dashed her head against the ground. It didn't hurt. Nothing did. In fact, she felt utterly numb as Hugh gripped her to him. He drew her away from the colonel, who moaned and growled in protest as Lord Thornton tried to give him aid.

"Carrigan," she said with a gasp. "He's been injured."

"He is fine. We came upon him shortly after, and he and Sir went to fetch soldiers at the barracks while Thornton and I split up to find you," Hugh said, leading her toward the curricle. "I don't think I've ever run so fast in my life," he added with a huff of breathless laughter. But she couldn't smile at his jest.

"I'm so sorry, Hugh, I had no idea. All this time, everyone believe you'd ruined Eloisa when it was...I can hardly think it, let alone utter it." The upheaval was catching up to her; she began to sway. And shiver. She was freezing, covered in mud and snow, every last inch of her damp.

Hugh tore off his greatcoat and wrapped it around her shoulders. "Let's not speak of it now." He pulled her closer, his arms rubbing her back vigorously, as if to warm her. It worked. His proximity helped too.

Shouts and whistles rang out from the southern edge of the park, where the horse guard barracks were located along the Knightsbridge Turnpike.

Audrey clutched Hugh by the elbow. "You need to go. They'll arrest you—"

"I'm not going anywhere. Thornton and I will explain what happened here, and Sir Gabriel will vouch for me too. He knows I've done nothing." He rested his forehead against hers. "It's over, Audrey."

Tears pricked her eyes as the tips of their noses brushed together, then apart. She exhaled as he held her and dared to believe him.

TWENTY-TWO

I t was the third cravat of the morning, and Hugh's patience was deteriorating. Hugh stood in his dressing room, hands clasped behind his back, as his valet fussed with the neckcloth.

"If you do not settle on a knot, Basil, I will be forced to rip off both of your arms and beat you about the head with them."

His valet did not flinch at the violent promise. He was far too involved in producing the finest mail coach knot he'd yet to tie in his many years of service.

"We will need several more neckcloths, my lord. I saw one in the loveliest shade of ecru at Bealman's last week, the barest hint of embroidery to give it a bit of texture," Basil said, his hands flitting about Hugh's neck like a pair of frantic birds.

"Do not call me that."

"You are wasting your breath, *my lord*. There is now only one 'Sir' in this household, and he is currently being fitted for proper livery."

As Basil reached for a cravat pin, the door to Hugh's bedchamber punted open and cracked against the wall.

"I ain't gonna wear this dandy color, Baz. I'd rather dunk

m'self in the Thames and eat a lungful of river water than be seen in these frilly threads!"

Sir stalked into the dressing room wearing unfinished versions of a coat and trousers in pale robin's egg blue, trimmed by silver tassels and embroidering. Hugh tried, but failed, to suppress a snort of laughter.

"It truly is an awful color, Basil," Hugh said. Sir tore off the pinned together sleeves and dumped them on the carpet.

"These are the established colors for Neatham livery!" Basil argued.

Hugh felt hot again, as he did every time he was reminded of the new state of his situation.

No longer was he Mr. Hugh Marsden, ward of the late Viscount Neatham, by-blow and blackguard disgrace. Sir Gabriel's man had found the recording of his father's and April Barlow's nuptials in the old parish church records. It matched with the certificate of proof April Barlow had possessed, tucked inside a box under her bed at the finishing school. And with no annulment on file, and April Barlow's verification that they did not dissolve their marriage before Fitzgerald married Joanna, the Committee of Privileges in the House of Lords had been forced to make the wholly irregular and extraordinary decision to declare Fitzgerald's second marriage bigamous, and to strip the title from Bartholomew.

"Things change, Basil. The Neatham livery can be another color." Hugh tugged at the finished cravat; it looked worse than the first, in his opinion. He stepped away from Basil before he could fuss any further.

"What color do you like, Sir?" Hugh asked.

"That is not how things are—"

The boy cut Basil off. "Green. Like the moss what's on rocks when the tide goes out."

Hugh grinned at Sir's sudden change of spirits. "Very well, green it is. Tell the tailor and be done with it."

Basil glared at the boy as he whooped and ran off. Hugh left the dressing room, forgoing the morning coat his valet tried to chase him with.

"I know you are in raptures about this change in our circumstances, Basil, but please understand, you are alone in your ecstasy," Hugh said as he left his bedchamber. He needed a drink, and he didn't care that it was only noon.

"I am not completely unsympathetic, my lord," Basil said, following him with less vigor now. "I'm quite aware that your rise in fortune did not come about without a great deal of turmoil. For that, I am deeply sorry."

The old snob sounded sincere, and Hugh felt a twinge of remorse for threatening to rip off his arms. As vexing as his valet was, he was steadfast and loyal, and he took no pleasure in the disgrace of Bartholomew and Lila Neatham. Neither did Hugh. He abhorred Barty, and after Lila tried to shoot him, Hugh didn't quite like the wife either. But total and complete ruination would be transferred onto their blameless young sons, and for that, Hugh was sorry.

Barty had not protested the Committee of Privileges's decision. The findings were irrefutable. Not only had April kept the certificate of her marriage to the viscount, she had also kept a copy of the parish record of Hugh's birth. The decision of the House of Lords was final. Objecting would never have worked to Barty's benefit, not with so much evidence in favor of Hugh —not to mention with the posthumous charges of murder brought against Thomas. There had been too much scandal already, and Barty's family was utterly tarnished. Too damaged to withstand the scrutiny, by far.

In Hyde Park, Thomas had fired off his shot before Hugh could even grip Thornton's pistol. By some miracle, neither he nor Thornton had been struck. Hugh's answering shot had flown true, and the lead ball had burrowed into his chest. Thomas lived long enough to confess to the murders of Eloisa Neatham and Lady Reed, and in the presence of the soldiers Sir and Carrigan had fetched from the barracks, no less. There had not been enough life left in Thomas for him to elaborate about why he'd killed Eloisa, or anything having to do with the child, and in the end, that might have been a blessing—at least for the child.

The correspondence with Mrs. Susan Smith that April Barlow had kept at her finishing school led Hugh to a small town in Gloucestershire, where Eloisa and her five-year-old daughter, Rosalie, had been living under false names and circumstances. Apparently, Susan Smith was a widow. Her close friends had been caring for Rosalie while her mother was in London to see to some "family business", or so Mr. and Mrs. Bailey had been told. The farmer and his wife already had three children of their own, but when they learned of Eloisa's death, they petitioned with Hugh to continue raising Rosalie. Hugh was in no position to deny them. To be raised in the countryside, sheltered from the truth of her birth would be the kindest of prospects. The Bailey family were good people and truly seemed to care for the little girl, and though they insisted it wasn't necessary, Hugh would financially take the girl on as his ward. She would want for nothing. Except, of course, her mother.

As for Lady Reed's murder, Hugh and Audrey, before they'd parted ways after the incident at Hyde Park, had pieced together what must have happened.

Thomas told Audrey that he'd seen and spoken to Eloisa at some point in the days before the soiree, whereupon Eloisa must have mentioned her plan to visit Lady Reed. Thomas would have known about the soiree, having been invited to it, but Eloisa had not. He'd followed her there with the smoke device he'd pilfered from the supplies designated for the military review. He'd seen the crowd not as a deterrent, but as an opportunity for chaos.

After speaking to Lady Reed the next morning, he must have become convinced that Eloisa confessed to the marchioness about Thomas and the child she'd born. So, he had silenced Lady Reed too. And when Audrey started asking questions about the gold leaf charm at the military review, Thomas must have realized his was missing from his sidearm, and that the duchess, who had found Eloisa's body, knew something. Appropriately, he'd panicked.

A part of Hugh had wished Thomas had lived long enough to hang for all his crimes, but at least his confession had exonerated Hugh.

"It will take me some time to grow accustomed to everything that has happened, Basil. I only ask for your patience," he said as he descended the stairs to the ground level. His timing was pure shite.

As he came off the last step, Mrs. Peets opened the front door, admitting Sir Gabriel Poston into the foyer.

"Oh, good, you're in," Sir Gabriel bellowed, handing over his walking stick and hat to the cook, who fumbled them.

"We will also need competent footmen," Basil whispered to Hugh as he walked by to help Mrs. Peets.

"Neckcloths and footmen. The list is growing," Hugh muttered, gesturing the magistrate into his study.

Many of the Neatham household staff had given their notices, Hugh had learned in the days following the upheaval. Only the butler and housekeeper and some grooms had stayed on; the rest had been unwilling to be associated with such scandal. If only Hugh, too, could give his notice and be on his way.

Unfortunately, he could not disclaim or renounce the title. It belonged to him, for better or worse.

"Whisky?" Hugh asked the magistrate as he was already pouring himself one.

"It's noon."

"So?"

Sir Gabriel grumbled, and Hugh took that for a yes. He handed the glass to the magistrate, who tossed it down his gullet.

"There is no point delaying. Best to be out with it," he said as Hugh moved to pour his guest another. "You are relieved from your duties at Bow Street, effective immediately."

The words landed the same as a fist to the gut. He had anticipated this but had not fully allowed himself to think on it. These last few weeks, every time Hugh arrived at Bow Street, Sir Gabriel had told him to sod off and get his affairs in order. But there had been a look in the magistrate's eye that had hinted that it was more than just a temporary lull in his duties.

"I am a damn good officer," Hugh said now, then downed his whisky in a single gulp.

Sir Gabriel scrubbed a palm over his moustache and chin. "You are one of my finest, but you are now viscount, and viscounts are not Bow Street officers."

Bloody hell. Hugh set down his whisky glass, and with more restraint than he'd ever shown, managed not to punch a hole in the wall.

"I never wanted this," he said, unable to look at Sir Gabriel. "I'm not qualified or prepared at all. It was never supposed to be mine—the estate, the land, the tenants. How am I to be steward of something I hold such bloody disdain for?"

If there had been any way at all around exposing Barty's illegitimacy, Hugh would have done it, and gladly. But Thomas's motive to kill his sister hinged entirely upon it.

"I don't imagine you held any great respect for the criminals you arrested in your time at Bow Street," Sir Gabriel said, "and yet you always followed proper procedure. You never let emotion or prejudice stand in the way of your duty."

"I made plenty of mistakes," he said, thinking of Fournier and how he'd arrested the duke for a murder he had not committed. Hugh had observed Miss Lovejoy's torn nails, received as she'd fought off her attacker, and yet he'd failed to observe that the duke had no defense wounds upon him. His hatred for the ton had blinded him.

"Don't I know it!" Sir Gabriel laughed. "But my boy, mistakes are not made with intention, and you have always been unswerving in your intention to do what is right." He came up to Hugh and clapped him on the shoulder in a show of either support or commiseration. "You are exactly the sort of gentleman the Neatham title needs at this time. You will give it the same dedication you gave me at Bow Street."

It was both a vote of confidence *and* a direct order. Hugh shook his head and grinned. "Yes, sir," he said, pouring himself another whisky.

"Good. I often have need of a contact with influence, you know," Sir Gabriel said. "You will hear from me again, don't worry."

He walked the magistrate back into the foyer, and as they entered, a light rap came at the front door. Basil had stationed himself there with Sir Gabriel's hat and stick, and now whisked open the door as well. A pair of inquisitive, dark blue eyes connected with Hugh's. The spring of his pulse was immediate. Audrey's lips bowed into an unreserved smile, then smoothed again when she saw the magistrate.

"Ah, Your Grace," Sir Gabriel said merrily, though he took a furtive glance toward Hugh, as if savoring the moment of finding the duchess on his doorstep.

"Good morning, Sir Gabriel," she replied as she and her maid entered the foyer. "Have I called at an inconvenient time?"

"No," Hugh answered just as the magistrate said the same.

"Not at all, I was just on my way." He accepted his stick and hat, but then, with a clearing of his throat and a cocked brow, continued. "Your Grace, I find myself in a most unusual position."

Audrey looked between Hugh and Sir Gabriel. "What position is that, Sir Gabriel?"

"The one in which I feel obliged to thank a lady of the peerage for her assistance in an investigation. Your observations regarding Colonel Trenton were indeed correct."

A stiff wind could have knocked Hugh over. By her look of surprise and her parted lips, the duchess felt the same way. He had never once heard the chief magistrate thank a woman for her help in anything. Hell, he wondered if he'd ever thanked any of his officers or constables.

"I was happy to assist," Audrey replied, the apples of her cheeks coloring with pleasure.

Sir Gabriel tipped his hat before leaving. Basil ushered Greer toward the sitting room, to await her mistress. Hugh and Audrey remained in the foyer, an awkward silence blooming.

They had not seen each other since the night in Hyde Park. He'd taken her home to Violet House, where the duke had swept her away for care. Hugh called on her the following afternoon, but she hadn't been receiving. A few more weeks passed, but there was always something keeping him from Curzon Street. Namely, the duke. Who was now one of Hugh's peers. As was Audrey.

"I should have sent a note ahead," she said just as he blurted out, "Would you like something to eat?"

He wasn't sure where the offer came from; he wasn't even hungry. And he ought to have offered her tea, not food. But as

Audrey blinked and pursed her lips against a grin, he realized why he'd said it. To keep her here, with him, for at least a little while.

"That depends. What have you got?"

"I haven't a clue." He nodded toward the kitchen. "Shall we go nettle Mrs. Peets?"

"Viscounts aren't supposed to nettle," she replied.

He held out an arm, gesturing toward the back of the house. "I suppose I'm not your typical viscount."

TWENTY-THREE

Not her typical viscount, indeed.

Audrey walked with Hugh to the kitchen of number 19 Bedford Street, wondering when he planned to quit the modest home and move to Kensington Square. The notion sent a strange curl of unease through her. Picturing Hugh moving about Neatham House didn't feel as natural as picturing him here, in these small but charming rooms. Picturing him as a viscount didn't feel quite right either. But he was. He was now a peer, and surely, things must change because of it.

She supposed that was one of the reasons she had avoided writing him or paying a call the last month and a half. Audrey had told herself that she was simply giving him time to adjust, for things to settle a bit. The tumult of solving Eloisa's murder, of killing his younger brother, and then, of being named rightful heir to the Neatham title, had to have been overwhelming. There was nothing Audrey could have done to help him acclimate, so she'd left him alone.

But in the quiet of the nights, when she lay in bed, unable to sleep, she would allow the real reason to gain a small foothold. Worry and doubt chased good sense straight out of her head when she thought of Hugh, which was far too often.

He was now viscount. Wealthy and powerful, his world was about to expand and fill with droves of eligible young ladies. And Audrey...well, she was slightly older and very much off the market.

For now.

The narrow hall to the back of the house terminated at a door, and when Hugh pushed it wide, the savory scents of herbs and roasted meat enveloped them.

"Oh! I wasn't expecting ye back here, my lord," the cook, Mrs. Peets, said as she jumped to attention at the cookstove.

Hugh pulled up short, and Audrey suspected that it was the form of address. *My lord.* He wouldn't be accustomed to hearing it. Strangely enough, as irregular as it felt to picture him mingling among the ton, hearing him called my lord seemed entirely natural. He had the weighty presence of a man of the peerage. He always had.

"Really, Mrs. Peets, I come to the kitchen on a regular basis. You've never been surprised to see me here before."

Just then, his valet, Basil, rushed in on their heels. "My lord, it is not customary for his lordship to enter the servants' rooms—"

"Out!" Hugh barked. The cook and valet startled with small leaps, and Audrey joined them.

"But my lord," Basil pleaded.

"Out!" he shouted again, though louder.

"My stew..." the cook started to say but when met with Hugh's glare, she dropped her protest and summarily fled the kitchen with Basil.

Hugh growled under his breath and pulled at his cravat as if he were suffocating.

"Why is this house so bloody hot? It's like a Turkish bath in here," he grumbled as he went to the back door and threw it open. The April sun washed the tiles at his feet.

Audrey crossed her arms before her and approached him. "What has happened?"

It wasn't like him to fuss and complain, and it wasn't overly warm in the house either. Hugh leaned a broad shoulder against the door frame, staring out into the small plot of back lawn, bordered by a narrow lane. "I've been relieved of my post at Bow Street."

Audrey's stomach dove. Compassion for him, and a glint of outrage, brought her to his side. She stopped short of laying a hand on his shirtsleeve. "I'm sorry. I know how much you love your work."

He'd told her how much he'd valued it before, and why. Having been exiled from his own family after the death of his father, ostracized as a villainous, good-for-nothing ward, he'd thrown himself into a new world, one of hard work, of seeking justice and punishing those who deserved it. Now, after she'd at last learned the truth about Eloisa's ruination, Audrey could understand Hugh's deeper longing, his truer motivation to lock up criminals.

It wasn't too difficult to parse why she had come to love working alongside him, solving the riddles of a handful of crimes this past year. It gave her a sense of purpose, of consequence. Audrey had always felt apart from her peers, and not just due to her ability to read the memories of objects. She had always longed for something more, something of significance. She had longed for something that made her feel alive. And she had come to realize that she never felt more alive than when she was working to solve an inquiry.

Or when she was with Hugh.

Before, she might have felt a tickle of guilt for thinking such a thing. But it didn't come this time. Philip had been closed off to her, ever since confessing his plan to disappear into the Continent; to leave her, his title, his duties, his whole life behind. She'd tried to broach the subject a few times over the last few weeks, but he had not wanted to discuss it. Audrey was hopeful he wouldn't go through with it; maybe he'd seen reason and changed his mind. But, even if he did choose to stay, things had altered between them. Gone a bit sour on the vine. Audrey simply didn't trust him as much as she used to, and it left her feeling bereft.

Hugh glanced at her. "I haven't the first idea how to be viscount."

"That's not true," she said. "You were raised by one."

"Always believing I was a cheaper version of him," he bit off, his jaw tight.

She'd had enough. Impetuously, she reached for his forearm and pinched it. He pushed off the door frame, glaring at her and rubbing his arm. "What the devil was that for?"

"For being stupid," she answered. Hugh turned to face her fully, arms crossing as though ready to meet her in a verbal sparring. "You are infinitely wiser than Bartholomew, not to mention honest and principled. You might not take pleasure in being a peer or for needing to change the direction your life was traveling before, but you have a duty. People are depending upon you, whether you like it or not. Bow Street officer or viscount, it doesn't matter. You are needed. Now, I won't hear another word about how you are inferior or second-rate, do you hear me?"

Audrey drew a long breath, and only then realized the extent of her diatribe. Warmth flooded up her neck, to her cheeks and the tips of her ears while Hugh continued to stare down at her, his lips parted. Then, the corner of his mouth quirked. "You are lovely when you blush."

"Don't compliment me, I was trying to be harsh "

Hugh fought to hold back his grin, but it was a losing battle. Audrey swatted his arm but retracted it quickly. Touching him could be dangerous. He was sinfully handsome. There was no getting around that fact. Thick dark hair, a strong nose and chin, full mouth, and fathomless sable eyes that always seemed to hold some shadowy sadness. Audrey was not immune to these things, and neither would any other young lady be. The taint of his laborer status would take some time to come off, but he was now titled, wealthy, and single. He'd be expected to take a wife.

She edged her heels back along the tiles, away from the open kitchen door. Away from Hugh. Distance always helped to ease the unrelenting weaving of her stomach and chest, her very blood it seemed. Audrey approached the stew pot on the cookstove and peered inside, to the bubbling concoction of vegetables and beef.

Behind her, the door closed. "That was the closest thing to an apology I've ever heard Sir Gabriel make, you know." Grateful for the change of subject, Audrey picked up the wooden spoon Mrs. Peets had abandoned and stirred the stew. "He was impressed by you."

"Reluctantly impressed, you mean," she said with a small shake of her head. "He hated admitting I was right about Colonel Trenton."

"He certainly did hate to admit it, but trust me," Hugh joined her at the stove. "If he was unhappy with your meddling, he would have blistered your ears."

She paused the spoon's rotation and balked at him. "Meddling? Might I remind you that I helped prove you innocent?" She began to stir again, splashing the contents against the side of the pot. "I was *aiding*, not meddling."

Hugh placed his hand on hers, stilling the spoon. "My

supper isn't arguing against that fact," he said, "and neither am I. Audrey—"

She slipped her hand out from underneath his and stepped back, away from the stove.

"The truth is," he said, his eyes following her skittering motion. "I am indebted to you."

"No," she said with a shake of her head. "You are never in my debt. I helped because I..." Goodness, it was warm in here after all. She licked her lips and finished. "Care."

During the several moments of silence that followed, Audrey questioned if she should have been so honest. But under Hugh's softening stare, she couldn't bring herself to regret it.

Still, it was time to get to the point of her visit.

"I've come for a reason. To welcome you into society and to give you this." She withdrew the square of heavy cardstock from her skirt's pocket. It was an invitation to her upcoming spring soiree, and it would be the only event held at Violet House before she and Philip quit London for the summer months. Or perhaps before Philip quit England altogether. She didn't want to think on that just now though.

"I'm not sure I will be able to attend," Hugh said after a mere glance at the invitation. He set it on the scarred wood of the kitchen table, treating it as he might a drowned rodent found in Mrs. Peets's pot of cream.

Audrey was not surprised at his reluctance. "You must have received a dozen or more like it by now. You've turned them all down, I imagine."

"I'm rather busy."

He wouldn't look at her, and instead began to fill a well-charred kettle on the stove with water. A viscount, making his own tea. Audrey bit her lower lip. This would certainly take some time.

"You will continue to be besieged," she warned. "I don't think you quite comprehend just how manipulative and commanding the mothers of young ladies who are of marriageable age can be."

It had been meant as a joke, and perhaps a way to untangle her own discomfort over the thoughts that had plagued her since news of his ascension. But Hugh did not smirk at her. Instead, he held her gaze and said, "I have no interest in finding a viscountess, Audrey."

She wished the pronouncement didn't make her so happy. It was wrong, wanting him to stay a bachelor. She had no right. And yet when he reached for her hand, this time, she didn't move away.

"This is becoming more complicated," he said, his attention on her hand, on running his ungloved fingers along hers, encased in silk. They traveled forward and back, over and across her knuckles with gentle reverence.

"It is," she whispered. "I shouldn't have come."

She tied to pull her hand back, but he held firm.

"The problem isn't your coming." His meandering fingers ascended to the lip of her glove. He breached it, and the coarse pads of his fingers brushed her skin. Heat sparked everywhere. "The problem is your leaving. I want you to stay with me."

Her heart paced faster as Hugh, almost absentmindedly, freed the two pearl buttons on her glove. He peeled the silk from her hand, from her fingertips, and then, Audrey watched in breathless wonder as he lifted her bare hand to his lips. He laid her inner wrist to his mouth, kissing her delicate skin.

"I want that too," she said. "If we are discreet..."

But he shook his head, short and abrupt as if it gave him pain. "I want you more than I've ever thought possible, but not as my secret. It was how my father treated my mother, how he in a way, treated me. It isn't right. Or honorable, and if I'm not mistaken, you think I'm rather honest and principled."

His lips stretched in a sly grin as his next kiss burrowed into the center of her palm. An answering fire kindled in the center of her chest, consuming the oxygen in her lungs.

"I also said you were stupid," she nearly gasped.

He laughed, nuzzled her hand once more, then lowered it. But he did not release her. "I am that. Undoubtedly, for I would rather have you in my life and not be able to touch you, than not have you in it at all."

"Hugh—" She stopped. Swallowed hard. Then shook her head. "I feel like I'm going to burst into flames."

He gripped her hand tighter at her whispered confession, and his glinting eyes became banked embers. "So do I."

"What are we to do?" Audrey thought of Philip and his plan. Hugh was too principled to conduct an affair, but if he believed she were widowed... But no. She couldn't lie to him. With Hugh, she was almost compulsively honest.

"I don't have an answer yet," he said, beginning to slip her glove back onto her hand. "Perhaps the next time we meet, I will."

Hugh finished clasping the pearl buttons on her glove, then lifted her hand to his mouth again. He kissed the ridge of her knuckles, his gaze steady on hers. With a rush of clarity, Audrey knew her feelings. She loved him. It wasn't only desire or attraction, or the thrill of the few dangerous incidents they'd been involved in together. This man—whether he was a Bow Street officer or viscount, a by-blow or an heir—had captured her whole heart.

And she was more fearful than ever that she was destined to lose him.

~

Thank you for reading Penance for the Dead and for continuing the Bow Street Duchess Mystery series! The fifth book in the series, FATAL BY DESIGN, is scheduled to release October 21, 2023, and is available for pre-order now!

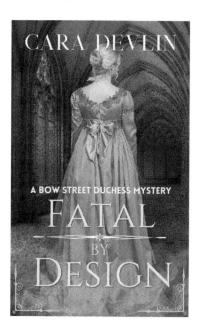

About the Author

Cara is an author, history lover, and Netflix junkie. She loves to read and write across genres, but her heart is reserved for romantic historical fiction and mystery. When she's not writing, she's freelance editing, driving her kids everywhere, burning at least one side of a grilled cheese, or avoiding doing laundry.

Also by Cara Devlin

Made in the USA
Monee, IL
26 May 2023

34684028R00139